CALL OF THE DEEP

J. C. McKenzie

Willa flapped her arms and tried to correct her balance, but it was too late. Her body hit the ocean with an icy slap. Her forehead struck a rock. Pain lanced across her face.

The water swirled around her, angry and dark. Her arms flailed as she tried to find a rhythm with her legs to stay afloat. She lacked control. The cold chopped at her face, and she gulped down seawater. No! This wasn't supposed to happen.

The water continued to crash against her, slamming her body into the rocks. Her head smacked a jagged edge and her vision, already poor in the fading light, narrowed, until only darkness and one thought remained.

Her body began to float upward. She opened her mouth to take a breath and quickly shut it. Her throat contracted and awareness flittered back. Her body had contorted into an awkward position with her torso arched forward and her limbs back, like the air trapped in her lungs fought to get out.

PRAISE FOR NOVELS OF
J. C. MCKENZIE

The Call of Corvids
"This is a fascinating read that brings together a world that has been marred with fae wars" ~ Fresh Fiction

Cormorant Run
"CORMORANT RUN by J. C. McKenzie is an amazing dystopic science fiction read that will have you mesmerized from the first word to the last."
~ Fresh Fiction

The Night House
"From the very first page till the very end I was hooked on this book and read it in less than one day...it had everything you could want from a story romance, secrets, lies, suspense, surprises and more."
~ Paranormal Romance Guild

Shift Happens
"SHIFT HAPPENS has excitement, intrigue and lots of danger. I love the whole cast of characters and how they played a part in the story" ~ Fresh Fiction

Beast Coast
"I loved this book as much as the first. There are secrets, surprises, and all manner of supernaturals."
~ Paranormal Romance Guild

Carpe Demon

"The story keeps the adrenaline pumping and spine tingling tension building throughout the story with well written scenes full of vivid details that capture the imagination and make it easy for the reader to become engrossed..." ~ Literary Addicts Book Community

Shift Work

"It's a terrific series and if you like supernatural reads, with a side of romance, the sort with solid and intense plots, gripping and very real dangers, hard choices, supernatural people some of whom can be selfish, cruel and bloodthirsty...You'll be hooked."
~ Jeannie Zelos Book Reviews

Beast of All

"This time out, J. C. McKenzie has outdone herself with high-velocity action, soul deep emotions and one of those finishes that you want to replay over and over!"
~ Tome Tender

Dangerous Dreams

"This new world promises to be an adventurous one full of snark, passion, thrills, romance, danger and wonderful characters and I can't wait to read the next one." ~ Stormy Vixen Reviews

Dangerous Liaisons
"Loved this story and loved Raf and strong, stubborn Lara and I can't overlook Lara's dragon who brought humor to this story." ~ Paranormal Romance Guild

The Good Griffin
"THE GOOD GRIFFIN is as addictive as a double shot of espresso, only without any of the withdrawal symptoms." ~ N. N. Light

BOOKS BY J. C. MCKENZIE

CALL OF THE DEEP

J. C. McKenzie

COPYRIGHT INFORMATION

Call of the Deep

Contact Information: jcmckenzie@jcmckenzie.ca

Cover Art: CReya-tive Book Cover Design

Publishing History:

First JCM Publications Edition, 2021

First Faery Rose Edition, 2014 (The Shucker's Booktique)

ISBN: (print): 978-1-990143-16-8

ISBN: (ebook): 978-1-990143-17-5

AUTHOR'S NOTE

This book was originally titled *The Shucker's Booktique* and published by The Wild Rose Press in 2014. Though large portions of the original story remain, this book has been heavily revised.

*This story is dedicated to the ocean lovers
who see magic in every wave.*

On the twilight sands of summer, I met the ocean's soul.

— ANGIE WEILAND-CROSBY

CHAPTER
ONE

"At the beach, life is different."

— SANDY GINGRAS, *HOW TO LIVE*
AT THE BEACH

THIRTY YEARS AGO...

Skye left the heated sandstone rocks and slipped into the cool ocean water. The hot afternoon sun beat down from above. She loved this time of day, this season. Summer on the island was already full of memories of sun-baked pine needles, salt spray, and peeling bark from arbutus trees. But now she had much more to look forward to and enjoy.

Skye dove below the surface. The cold water flowed over her sun-warmed skin and pushed her long blond hair from her face. She felt along the algae and

1

starfish covered rocks until she found the familiar entrance. With strong kicks, she thrust forward, propelling herself through the narrow tunnel. She popped out on the other side in a secret cave, carved over time from waves and erosion.

Bringing her legs underneath her, she stood and let the ocean water drip from her body. She ran a hand along her hair to slick it back and keep the long blond strands from her face.

This place always smelled of wet dirt, ocean water and seaweed. The connection between scents and memories had always been strong with her, and images from her time previously spent in this cave came flooding back, heating her body with a different kind of warmth.

Memories of naked skin pressed to hers, sliding along her body. Limbs entwined. Lips locked.

Ecstasy.

She took a deep breath and blinked away the memories.

Little holes in the sandstone ceiling created by weather and roots let in air and bands of summer sunshine. Dotted rays danced along the damp stone and water like fairy light while the gentle waves traversed the tunnel and lapped at the slanted sandstone floor of the cave.

Though she hadn't spoken or made any sound, the man standing in the centre of the cave turned. The ethereal light streaming through the ceiling created a glowing halo around his platinum blond hair and made his ocean green eyes flash.

A lifetime of swimming in the ocean had sculpted his tall body to perfection. He'd arrived at their secret meeting place before her, and he wasn't wearing a thing.

He raked her body with his wicked gaze and purred like a siren. "My love."

She stepped from the water and into his warm embrace.

CHAPTER
TWO

"A day moves not from hour to hour but leaps from mood to moment."

— SANDY GINGRAS, *HOW TO LIVE*
AT THE BEACH

CURRENT DAY...

Willa Eklund toed the sandstone ledge with her boot, peered down the rocky cliff face and contemplated jumping. The churning ocean below beckoned, calling her to its freezing depths to play. Surely an ice-cold dip in the salt chuck would bring back some sense of feeling to her numb heart.

She shook her head.

Or hypothermia.

4

Dad had spent her entire youth cautioning her about proper water safety and the dangers of the ocean, and though he passed away years ago, she still heard his voice in her head as if he stood right beside her.

At around six degrees Celsius, the ocean surrounding Gabriola Island—Gabe to the locals—was an unpleasant place to frolic in the winter and spring months. Hypothermia would set in within thirty minutes if she didn't manage to pull herself from the frigid waters.

Salt air whipped at her face, cold and stinging, like memories of home.

Had Willa's aunt stood here? Had Aunt Jenny pondered jumping from this location? She'd sounded so happy on the phone the last time they spoke almost two weeks ago, telling a tale of skinny dipping in her youth just to feel alive and how they had so much to catch up on once Willa arrived.

Except her Aunt Jenny hadn't greeted Willa when she disembarked the ferry. She wasn't waiting in the small terminal's parking lot, either. She wasn't at work, nor was she in the living quarters above the quaint bookstore she owned.

If Aunt Jenny hadn't left keys with the coffee shop owner next door, Willa would've been stranded with no clue of how to proceed.

She still had no clue, but she couldn't go back to Vancouver. That life was over and good riddance.

Gabriola Island sat nestled between the much

larger Vancouver Island and the mainland of British Columbia in the Strait of Georgia. With a local population of around four-thousand, and nearly triple that in the summer with vacation properties, Gabe was known for its high percentage of working artists, grow-ops and a persistent rumour of an operating nudist colony. But none of those things kept Willa enthralled with the gulf island. No, the sandstone beaches and the arbutus and pine forests drew Willa like a moth to a flame.

Willa peered down at the churning ocean again. She wouldn't jump. She had too much left to figure out. She turned from the cliff's edge, her boot twisting in the damp moss lining the edge.

Rocks groaned. Loam filled the air and a chunk of the rock face fell away. Willa careened backward. She flailed her arms, trying to find her footing, but one blink and she was falling, weightless, suspended in the air before gravity kicked in and wrenched her toward the angry ocean below.

Willa hit the water awkwardly. Her shoulders struck first, then her head and back. Pain streaked through her body and cold water slapped her senses.

She sank below the surface. A wave-like pulse shot from her body. The cold seeped into her limbs, her head grew fuzzy and prickly. Her legs tingled. Dazed, she blinked to adjust to the underwater lighting. The dark serenity of the ocean oddly comforted her.

It should have scared the bejeezus out of her, but nope.

In addition to spending her life respecting the dangers of the ocean, she also devoted a lot of time to researching it. The ocean constantly plagued her mind and she sought ways to understand everything beneath its often-murky surface. But why did the icy depths appeal to her? Only death waited for her here.

She hadn't even turned thirty yet.

Her hair lazily flowed back and forth across her face. With a great kick of her legs, she pushed her body upward until her head broke the surface. She dragged in a deep breath of salty air and the tingling in her legs disappeared.

"Hey!" A man called out from the rocky shore. "Are you okay?"

Willa started paddling toward the shore. She might physically be fine, but she was beginning to have serious doubts about her sanity.

"Wow," the man spoke again when she got closer. She recognized him now. Officer Harris had been present when she'd reported Aunt Jenny missing.

"That was quite a fall." He stepped into the water, the gentle waves lapping at his boots. Tall, with broad shoulders and a narrow waist, Officer Harris had brown hair, matching brown eyes and a gentle smile. "I thought I was going to have to go in after you."

She accepted his outstretched hand and let him haul her out of the water.

"It was a fall...right?" His eyebrows pinched in, concern evident in his expression.

"Sure was." She rubbed her arms, but no amount of rubbing prevented the chill from seeping into her bones. Her teeth started chattering.

"Did you drive or walk here?" he asked.

"Walked," she managed to get out between her teeth.

"Did you lose your keys in the water?" he asked.

She patted her zipped up jacket pocket and felt the familiar lumps. At least she hadn't lost her keys. That would've made everything worse. She shook her head.

"That's lucky. More than a few people have lost their keys or wallets over that cliff's edge. I'll give you a lift home. You need to get warm and dry before the storm sets in."

Willa glanced over her shoulder at the sky. Sure enough, angry dark clouds moved toward the small island.

With a deep breath, she let Officer Harris lead her away from the pebbled beach, and ignored the itching sensation running along her back, teasing her to turn around and go back into the water.

CHAPTER
THREE

"We go with the currents, plan around the tides, follow the sun."

— SANDY GINGRAS, *HOW TO LIVE
AT THE BEACH*

Bang! Bang! Bang!

Willa bolted upright in bed. The white sheets clung to her damp tank top and shorts. Her gut clenched, and foreboding trickled down her spine like sweat. The shapes of the furnishings in her aunt's second floor guest room slowly materialized as her eyes adjusted to the dark night. Rain pounded against the bedroom window, and the tall fir trees groaned in the gale force winds outside. She closed her eyes and inhaled the lingering smells of sea breeze that seemed to perpetually cling to the air.

The thunder must've woken her.

She dropped back onto the soft pillows and let sleep slide over her body again.

Bang! Bang! Bang!

Willa flung back the bed sheets and set her feet on the rustic wood flooring. That wasn't thunder. The loud thumping sounded like someone slamming their fist against the bookstore's front door downstairs.

Who the heck would come over at...Willa glanced at the bedside clock, and the ugly green lights glared back at her. Who the heck would knock on the door of Bound to Please at three in the morning? On a weeknight?

The banging continued, and she lurched from the bed. Maybe someone had found her aunt. It had been two weeks now since anyone heard from her.

Maybe Aunt Jenny knocked on the door or maybe the cops stood on the landing, preparing to deliver bad news.

Dread dropped in her gut like lead and twisted.

She threw on her robe, her heart thudding in her chest, and raced down the stairs to the bookstore below. When she reached the shop's entrance, she flipped the three deadbolts and flung the heavy oak door open.

It wasn't her aunt.

Or the police.

A giant hurricane of a man stood in front of her. She should've looked through the peephole.

Easily standing over six and a half feet, his wide shoulders took up most of the doorway. Flashes of lightning illuminated porcelain, almost translucent skin, and dark, stormy eyes that appeared to contain gray thunder clouds changing to the deep blue of an angry ocean. Ink-black hair, dripping with rainwater, plastered his chiseled features and added to his severe, angular face.

His eyes widened briefly, then narrowed to study her. He hesitated before stepping forward.

Willa squeaked and slammed the door closed.

Or at least tried to. He stuck his foot out and the door bounced off his shoe to rebound into her face with an audible crack.

She flapped her arms in the air like a nubile hatchling before she hit the floor. Her head smacked the bookstore's tiles. Her vision swam and she clutched her face. Pain shot through her nose and the back of her head.

"Ooooooo," she groaned.

She prodded the tender skin. No blood. She continued probing the bridge of her nose. Pain flared, but not ridiculously.

Okay, probably not broken.

The man slipped into the bookstore and shut the heavy door against the raging storm outside. He knelt beside her and placed his hand gently on her shoulder. "Are you okay? I didn't mean to frighten you."

His fingers tingled on her skin, shooting feathery wisps of energy down her arm. She closed her eyes and enjoyed the sweet vibrations as they radiated through her. Delicious and unique.

The man's gaze widened again, and he snatched his hand back. He dropped his gaze to scan her body.

Well, this was awkward. With her robe flung open and transparent white tank top beneath, he could see everything in the streaks of lightning. She needed to change.

Wait. This guy had practically barged into the bookstore in the middle of the night and now she lay flat on her back, possibly concussed. Her outfit was the least of her concerns right now. What was this man doing in Jenny's bookstore?

Yet no words came out of her mouth. She just lay there, dazed, and stared. Guess she knew what her fate would be if she ever found herself in a horror movie.

"I'll get you something cold. You should stay still." The man got up from his crouch and walked through the bookstore to the kitchen at the back of the building. He never hesitated when navigating through the store. He'd been here before. And often.

"Jenny?" he called out loud enough for Willa to hear him from where she remained sprawled on the floor. "You here?"

While she continued to listen to him call out for

her missing aunt, Willa sighed and struggled to sit up. She didn't want to remain sprawled on the floor like a stunned snow angel, glowing in the light from the raging storm outside.

The house creaked and groaned with the wind and the man's movement through the house. As he walked back into the store's main room, he ran his hand along the book bindings. She did the same thing. The smell of old paper and the feel of the worn leather bindings comforted her almost as much as spending time watching the ocean.

The man faltered when he reached her, as if unsure of how to proceed. She'd managed to prop herself up and close her robe in an attempt at modesty.

He seemed to collect himself and walked around her to flick on the last of the lights. The artificial bulbs banished the ethereal glow in the room.

Finished with the lights, he knelt by her side and tenderly pressed a bag of frozen peas to the back of her head. "Here you go."

She reached back to take control of the peas and her hand brushed his hand. His skin zapped her with static shock. She jerked back.

"Easy," he said. "You took quite a spill."

The coolness from the frozen peas soothed the pulsing ache in her head. None of this would've happened if he hadn't jammed his foot in the door. For some reason, though, the man's presence put her at ease instead of setting off alarms. As a former city-dweller, that wasn't right. Usually, she viewed strange men with suspicion, and certainly a healthy dose of caution. They could be serial killers for all she knew.

She settled on glowering at him while continuing to hold the peas to the back of her head.

"I'm not here to hurt you," he said. "I'm sorry I gave you a fright."

That's probably the same thing serial killers said before they struck.

"Why are you here?" she asked.

"Looking for Jenny. Is she around?"

"No, she's not." Her muscles tensed again. After a pause, she pushed his arms away and attempted to stand. She felt like a newborn colt getting up for the first time. Her legs shook and wobbled. He clasped his hands and rocked on the balls of his feet as he stayed in a crouched position.

"Do you know anything about that?" she asked. That's right, totally a good idea to interrogate a potential serial killer. *Awesome work, Nancy Drew.*

He dragged his attention away from her legs and straightened to stand beside her. "About what?"

"About where she is?" She flung her unruly mane from her face and wobbled again.

The man reached out to steady her. When his hand touched her arm, she squeaked and jumped back. There was definitely some weird tingling going on, as if he perpetually held a static charge.

He ran his hand through his wet hair and spoke

14

softly. "Why would I look for her here if I knew where she was?"

She pursed her lips and squeezed her body tight with her arms.

"We should take you to the doctor." He studied her again. "You don't look well."

At first, this man's intimidating presence had scared her. He was huge, mysterious, and banging his fist against her missing aunt's door at a god-awful time in the morning. But now she wanted to touch him, to feel that cool, sweeping energy when he touched her, like he left an imprint. She'd never felt anything like it before and the lust coursing through her veins scared her more than his size or the circumstances.

A deep ache resonated from her right temple and the back of her skull thudded painfully. Her thoughts zinged around in a muddled frenzy. He wanted to take her to a doctor, but maybe he should take her to a therapist instead.

The wind howled outside, followed by a flash of lightning and another crack of thunder. Under the store's lights, Willa took in more of the stranger's appearance. Old, faded jeans with ripped knees, from wear and tear not fashion, clung to his muscled thighs; a simple black long-sleeved shirt, one size too small, spanned his broad, muscular chest; and his scuffed, soil-sodden running shoes with untied laces tracked dirt into the store. The storm had victimized his clothing, and the drenched material dripped onto the tile flooring along with a trail of mud and leaves.

"I'm so sorry." She dragged her gaze away from his chest. If this man wanted to harm her, he had his chance when she lay flat on her back doing her best floor-tile impression. "You must be cold. Do you want something warm to drink or a towel?"

"I don't mind the cold." His voice blended with another rumble of thunder. "But I would enjoy a hot drink, if it's not too much of an inconvenience. Maybe you can tell me what's going on with Jenny."

Her dizzy spell over and her legs more stable, she nodded and walked to the back of the bookstore where the office, kitchen and one of the bathrooms were situated. "It's through here."

"I know. Jenny and I met often for tea."

Willa bit her lip. She'd had no idea her aunt had a male companion. A "special friend." Something hollowed out in her chest, leaving an empty stabbing pain. Everyone had a better love life than she did, even her reclusive, book-loving aunt.

"Sorry, I wasn't aware my aunt had a boyfriend. She never mentioned you. If you'll have a seat, I'll put the kettle on." She waved at the small dinette in the back room and walked to the kitchen counter to turn on the electric kettle. She didn't want to look at the man. She didn't want him to see her face and the longing that must be evident in her expression. She simply wanted someone to share her life with, and instead, she got burned.

When she reached for the kettle, a large smooth hand closed over her trembling one. A cool wave of energy flowed through her body from where his skin touched hers. She squeaked and jumped back half a step.

And bumped into a wall of muscle.

"I tell you what." The man spoke into her hair, causing shivers to dance down her body. "Why don't I get the hot drinks started and you get dressed?"

She looked down at her outfit and warmth spread across her face. Her robe had opened and her white tank top, already tight, remained transparent from the rain. Clutching the robe around her body, she skirted around the man to head for the stairwell. "Good idea."

The man wasn't looking at her. He stood stiffly at the counter and studied the kettle as if it contained all the secrets in the world, completely indifferent to her near naked state.

BRANCHES from the fir trees slapped against the window as another gust of wind rocked through the backyard of the house. In the dark, with only flashes of lightning to illuminate them, the branches looked like phantoms scratching to get in.

Willa shivered and went back to dressing. She settled for dark skinny jeans, and a flowy, mint green shirt. The clinking of mugs drifted upstairs as the mysterious stranger loitered downstairs supposedly making tea.

Absently, she ran a brush quickly through her long blonde hair. Her hair responded by poofing out to twice its thickness. Ugh. She knew better than to do that.

She surveyed the mess in the mirror. A hair tie would have to do. She snatched one from the dresser and quickly pulled her hair up. Her heart thudded in her chest as a personal timekeeper. With the amount of time she'd already taken, George would've been yelling at her by now.

Willa paused. Well, George hadn't wanted her in the end. She could take all the time she needed.

With one last look in the mirror, she spun around to walk downstairs. Her heartbeat picked up at the thought of looking into the dark, mysterious depths of the stranger's thundercloud eyes.

This guy might have the answers she sought about Aunt Jenny's disappearance, but he could also be the one responsible. Though the latter seemed unlikely, unless he moonlighted as an actor or was a sociopath, she still needed to be careful.

The heritage home groaned with each step on the hardwood stairs. Her aunt had spent a lot of money converting this old house into a trendy, profitable, book-selling business. Not an easy thing to do on a small island.

The charming three thousand square foot home had been built by a local merchant and shipwright. Since then, the home had passed through many hands and had been vacant since the 80s. Aunt Jenny bought it with inheritance money and entrenched herself in her job, always saying it didn't count as work when it was something she loved.

Something must've gone wrong. Bound to Please was Aunt Jenny's baby, her life, her world. She'd never abandon it. She'd never abandon Willa.

Willa's heart stopped its hard, anticipatory beating and sank a little in her chest. At the base of the stairs, she took a deep breath and prepared to launch into an excuse to usher the stranger out of her aunt's home with a promise to discuss things in the daylight. She didn't owe this man her time or any explanations. No matter how polite or good-looking he was, calling on someone at this time of night was inappropriate. She turned the corner and walked into the kitchen.

The stranger stood in the outline of the kitchen's window. When he fastened his steely gaze on her, his piercing storm-gray eyes flashed in unison with the borderline-cyclone outside.

She jerked to a stop and her breath snagged in her throat.

"There you are," he said. His gaze roamed her body and a slight smile tugged at his lips. "I made you herbal tea. I figured it was too late..." He glanced outside. "Or early, for anything caffeinated."

"Thanks. Smells good." She reached out and accepted the steaming cup. It slipped partially from her hands, and she groped at the mug before it fell to the ground. Clutching the handle, she dried the outside off with her shirt and glanced at the man. He was still soaked.

"You're still drenched," she said. "Are you sure I can't offer you a towel, or something? I don't think we have any clothes, er, big enough to fit you, but at least you could dry off."

His lips twitched. "I don't mind. I'll dry off soon enough."

"Okay..." Normally, she'd be annoyed at someone bringing so much water into the house, but the dripping effect somehow added to his striking appearance.

Silence stretched in the small kitchen as the storm thundered outside. The pine and loam smells from earlier were gone, replaced with herbal tea, and the dew of rainwater.

"My name is Willa." She stretched her hand out. "Jenny's niece."

He straightened from leaning against the counter and took a few strides forward before clasping her trembling digits with his enormous hulking hand. "Lon."

She sucked in a quick breath as another wave of heat flowed from the contact. "Lon?"

"Lon." He nodded. "Jenny's *friend*."

They stood and studied each other. Part of her didn't want this moment to end. She didn't want him to release her hand from his warm grip, but sadly, he did, and her arm fell to her side.

"Why don't we have a seat?" Lon suggested and lifted his chin toward the counter-height table and chairs a few feet away. "I'd like to hear about Jenny."

She nodded and took the seat closest to the door.

The man's confidence and his comfortable demeanor around Aunt Jenny's place might put her at ease, but he was still a stranger. She needed to keep reminding herself of that.

"You asked me where Jenny was," Lon said. He took the dish towel from the stove handle and placed it on the opposite seat before sitting down. The move so fluid, it came across well practiced. Interesting.

"Yes." She narrowed her eyes at him. "Do you know where she is?"

Lon sighed and glanced out the window again. "As I already pointed out, I wouldn't have come here looking for her if I knew she was elsewhere."

His words made sense, and a bit of her fear dissipated. The circumstances of his presence might be odd, but none of his actions indicated he was here to harm her. He'd come to see Aunt Jenny, but why visit her aunt at such an early hour?

Something wasn't quite right about him or this situation. Willa snapped her mouth shut and looked at the tabletop. She'd eaten oatmeal in this very spot this morning and had missed a spot when cleaning up.

A dull ache continued to throb behind her eyes. She shouldn't be surprised her head hurt. The door had smacked her in the face, she'd landed on hard tiles and earlier today she'd taken a tumble off that cliff into the ocean. Really, she should be surprised her brain still functioned.

She picked at the dried oatmeal and shook her head.

"Willa?"

"Hmm?" She continued to pick at the oatmeal. George would never stand for such uncleanliness.

"Willa?"

"Yes?" She glanced up and froze as the intensity of his gaze hit her.

"What's going on? What happened to Jenny?"

Her shoulders sagged and she gave up on the oatmeal, gave up on any hint of normalcy. She'd kept hoping this was some horrible dream, and her aunt would come waltzing through the door any minute.

Talking to the Royal Canadian Mounted Police, or RCMP for short, had been difficult, but admitting the truth to this stranger, this friend of her aunt's, made it feel even more real.

"She's missing." Her voice caught and her breathing hitched. Tears welled up and she squeezed her eyelids shut to prevent them from falling. No way would she cry in front of a stranger.

"Missing?" he asked.

She nodded, eyes still shut, and explained, "She's been missing for about two weeks. As far as we can tell, no one has seen or heard from her since her last customer, Tess McIntyre, left the shop on February twentieth. Aunt Jenny closed up shortly afterward and hasn't been seen since."

"And you believe this Tess?"

"Frankly, if Tess knew anything, the whole town would," Willa said. "I'm new to the island, but even the gossip from Tess's loose tongue has reached me. She told the RCMP she heard Aunt Jenny turn the lock to the front door after she left the shop. Aunt Jenny texted me the day before she went missing to tell me how excited she was to see me and to let me know if she was out when I arrived for whatever reason, she'd left a set of keys for me with the neighbour." Apparently, the ferry was often off-schedule, so Aunt Jenny had planned for all possible outcomes.

Well, almost all.

"And did she?"

"Yes. I wouldn't have gotten in the building if she hadn't. But it's all so odd. Why didn't she text me to explain where she went or why she couldn't meet me?"

His eyes, which had widened at first, now narrowed and studied her face. "And no one else has seen her?"

"No one. It's as if she vanished. No cell phone activity, no banking. Nada." Willa clasped her mug and bowed her head. Months ago, her aunt had offered her refuge after George left. Aunt Jenny was the only family member not telling her to suck it up, or that it was all her fault, or if she'd known how to take care of a man, he wouldn't have left. Her own mother suggested she crawl back to George and beg for a second chance.

Lon reached out and brushed her hand. "Who's Tess McIntyre?"

Gentle waves swooshed up her arms from the brief contact. She gaped at him before she recalled his question. Surely, such a tingling sensation wasn't normal. "J-just a regular customer who chats...chatted with my aunt. She's a bit of a town gossip, but her story checks out. After talking with Aunt Jenny, she purchased a book, and went to work. She's the receptionist in the RCMP building."

"Does Jenny have any known enemies?"

The look she gave him must've been answer enough, because he grunted and then drummed his fingers on his mug. Of course, Aunt Jenny didn't have enemies. How could anyone hate the unassuming woman?

"What about you?" she asked and met his thundercloud eyes. The skin on the hand he'd brushed had turned cold, yearning for him to repeat the gesture. She refused to look at his fingertips and studied his face instead.

"Sorry?"

"What's your alibi?" she asked, though, as time

progressed, Lon looked less like a suspect and more like an ally.

"Didn't we already establish I don't know anything?" His brows pinched together, making his face more angular. Outrage danced in the gray of his eyes. The expression contorted his translucent skin, and the flash of something unusual in his face made the neurons zing in her head. Her skin prickled as the tiny hairs on her neck stood up. She leaned forward and squinted, but the moment was gone.

I'm seeing things.

Willa clutched her mug and sat back in her seat. "You could've said that to throw me off. Maybe you came by to get something of my aunt's. Why are you here? It's a rather odd hour to visit a *friend*." Now, if that were true, if he came to hide evidence of a crime, confronting him was probably not one of her more brilliant ideas.

Lon's lip curled up. "That's ridiculous. I could've taken whatever I wanted when you knocked yourself out with the door. I came to visit Jenny."

"Then where've you been these last two weeks?" The island wasn't that big. Surely, she would've noticed him before now if he'd been in town, and surely, he would've already heard the news about Jenny's disappearance. News spread quickly in the small community.

Lon shifted in his seat. "Around."

"Around?" Unease flittered up her spine and

settled at the base of her skull. Maybe he really had come for something. Money, clothes. He certainly needed both.

"I travel a lot for work."

"And what kind of work is that?"

He paused and glanced outside. The storm had died down again, but from her aunt's stories, she knew the weather could settle for hours before starting again. "The eye of the storm," she'd say.

"I sell weather insurance."

Willa snorted. Some of her tea bubbled up her nose and she clasped a hand over her face. Liquid dribbled down to her mouth and her cheeks burned.

"Here," he said and passed her a napkin.

She snatched it out of his hand and cleaned off her face, wanting to die. She crumpled the napkin in her hand. "Thank you."

"My pleasure." He glanced at the window again, a tiny smile pulling at his lips before he pushed his chair away from the table. "I'm sorry for intruding on you in the middle of the night. I hope the authorities find Jenny, and if I hear anything, I'll let you know. She's a dear friend, and I'd never want anything bad to happen to her." He moved around the table before she could react to his words.

"Err," she said.

"I really must go." He took her hand, the non-snotty one, and slowly brought it to his face. He pressed his lips against her knuckles and warm tension replaced her apprehension. "It was a pleasure to meet you, Willa. I hope to see you again."

He walked straight for the bookstore's front door and had already closed it behind him before Willa stumble-ran to the front entrance.

"Wait!" she yelled as she flung open the door.

"How do I get a hold...?" Her question trailed off in the wind. Lon had disappeared into the night.

CHAPTER
FOUR

"We measure happiness by nothing we can hold...nothing we can catch."

— SANDY GINGRAS, *HOW TO LIVE
AT THE BEACH*

Willa didn't sleep for long. Soon enough, the light of the day teased her awake. The morning smelled fresh and clean with the tang of ocean breeze. Willa stretched in bed and enjoyed the sounds of nature. Wildlife always seemed louder after a storm, as if crying their defiance. Resident birds sang to greet the sunrise while the calm breeze teased the evergreen trees, and the waves gently lapped the shore nearby.

Steaming hot water ran over Willa as she turned her face into the shower spray. Usually, a shower in the morning helped her wake up and focus, but one image had replayed in her mind over and over again while she got ready for the day. A memory of storm gray eyes and a low rumbling voice. Her hands travelled from meticulously washing her hair to sliding down her neck to caress her breasts before slipping between her legs.

She froze. What was wrong with her? She didn't even know the man and he was probably banging her aunt.

Maybe she should've taken a cold shower.

With a groan, she turned off the water and flung back the shower curtain. Stepping out of the steaming shower, she toweled off before dressing in worn jeans and a faded long-sleeved shirt.

She shouldn't fantasize about a stranger, no matter how irregular he made her heart beat. Those stormy eyes ranging from dark gray to deep, ocean blue spelled trouble.

The serenity of the early morning beyond the window snagged her attention. The fir trees swayed in the wind and the horizon lightened to dark blue with the rising sun. The storm outside had died down. The ocean lost its rage and the wind ceased whistling. Willa cracked open the window a little for some fresh air. Only the sound of waves in the distance trickled into the room, flowing over her like a lover's hands, seductive and promising.

Now that the storm had ebbed, she shouldn't hear the ocean this far from the beach, but the call of the sea still teased her. She itched to visit the shore just to watch the play of the waves in the morning light.

That's how Willa knew she was truly losing her mind, and she didn't even care.

Willa padded down to the kitchen to make something hot to drink. Normally, she'd make coffee, but this morning, she craved the drink she'd shared with Lon last night. The spices still lingered on her tongue, bringing back the memory of her night-time visitor.

With her mug in one hand and her tablet in the other, she sat down to scan the news and check her e-mail. The shrill ring of the phone demolished the tranquil moment.

She plucked the old receiver from the wall. She used to make fun of her aunt for keeping the thing, with its tangled, extra-long, coiled cord. But now, as she handled the phone, reassuring warmth spread through her palm at the thought of her aunt. "Hello?"

"Willa." Her mom's blunt voice came through the connection as clear as the morning outside.

Willa winced. She needed a pep-talk from her mother about as much as she needed a hammer to the head. "Hi, Mom."

"Have you finished the month-end finances?"

"I just got here two weeks ago."

A pause. "I don't see your point."

"I'm not even sure I've found all the receipts,

invoices and bank statements. You know Aunt Jenny, she's not exactly the most organized. We're lucky she arranged for me to have access to the business accounts before she went missing." Willa picked at the fraying edge of her sleeve. "Which looks super suspicious to the cops, by the way."

"Did you have something to do with her disappearance?" Mom asked.

"What?" Willa jerked her head back and stared at the phone until her brain cells could formulate one cohesive thought. "Why would you even ask that?"

"So that's a no?"

"Yeah, it's a no."

"Then you have nothing to worry about."

Honestly, if anyone was capable of offing another member of the family, it would be Mom. The woman was ruthless. The only reason Willa didn't suspect her was her thriftiness. Mom was simply too cheap to hire someone to do something she could do herself and if social media time stamps were accurate, Mom had spent the entire weekend with her sisters.

"Your aunt is a spineless dreamer," Mom continued. "You have a lot in common with my sister-in-law."

The insult would've stung had it been the first, or even second or third time Willa had heard it, but Mom held nothing back when it came to expressing her opinion about her youngest daughter. *Well, you and my sisters made me this way.*

"When can I expect you to e-mail them?" Mom asked.

"I'll try to get to them today."

"Don't try, do."

"Mom, I—"

"If you spent half the time doing as you were told instead of whining about a simple task, you'd probably have the job done by now."

Wow. "I wasn't whining. Have you heard anything about Aunt Jenny?"

Mom went silent on the other side of the line. Willa could imagine her clutching the cell phone with a death grip and pursing her injected lips. She'd have her long blond hair pulled back in a tight ponytail or bun.

Willa used to wonder what she'd done to piss off her mother so much. Now, Willa just wanted to be left alone.

Distance didn't make the heart grow fonder, it gave her breathing room. And perspective. The longer she spent away from her family, and out from under the thumb of her controlling mother, the more she saw the relationship for what it truly was.

Toxic.

Guilt stabbed at her chest. Of course, she'd learned about abusive relationships in school and read about them in books, but she never considered the possibility her own mother could harm her so much without lifting a finger.

"Are you so eager to foist your aunt's store on someone else?" her mom finally asked.

"I want to know Aunt Jenny is okay." Why did Mom find that so hard to believe?

"Humph. Well, we'll see about that. If you want to help your aunt, you'll do a better job of running her business. That bookstore turned a profit every year since she started, surprising for such a dilapidated place."

Though Willa couldn't actually see Mom, she could tell from her voice she wore her trademark sneer, the condescending one Willa had become so familiar with because she was often the recipient of it.

"Full of hippies and losers," Mom kept speaking. "I can smell the patchouli from here."

Rather judgemental of her. Willa had seen the pictures. Mom had a hippy-past but seemed Hell-bent on acting like it never happened.

That wasn't the only thing Mom struggled with. She'd never managed to say the name of the store, Bound to Please. Found it beneath her and her more sophisticated sense of humour. Though Willa wasn't aware she had any sense in that department. If she did, Willa never saw it.

"You need to report your sales to me daily," Mom ordered.

"I'll send an e-mail," Willa replied.

Mom had no business or right to meddle or keep tabs on Aunt Jenny's store but sending the reports might provide Willa with a reprieve from her nagging and sharp tongue.

"Yes, you will. And stop sounding so upset about it. You should thank me for letting you stay there instead of sending one of your sisters. They would've been more capable, but they have families. They have lives." She snorted.

And now Mom wanted to take credit for Willa's presence at the bookstore, like this was her idea all along. Like she could send one of Willa's sisters in her place when Willa's name was on the business accounts alongside Aunt Jenny's.

Mom's arrogance grated on Willa's nerves. Mom hadn't sent her here. Nor did Mom have any say in who ran the store or how. The audacity. Mom was trying to rewrite events to make her look better and suit her secret agenda. Whatever that was.

"It's not like you had anything worth sticking around for in Vancouver," Mom continued. "Not after George left you."

"Mom, seriously?" Willa closed her eyes, knowing instinctively where this conversation headed, yet powerless to stop it. She never should've let Mom push her into dating George in the first place. It didn't make either of them happy, and now that she was out of the relationship, she saw how wrong George was for her, how much of a shell she had become of her true self.

And Willa let it happen. That hurt almost as much as all the other crap George made her feel.

"What?" Mom said. "If you knew how to keep a man, you wouldn't be almost thirty and alone. Just watch. If you don't change your ways, you'll end up like your spinster aunt. Why can't you be more like your sisters? They never had problems keeping their men."

Willa took a deep breath. What was the point? In the past, she'd tried to defend herself and her choices, only to get steamrolled by Mom's indomitable will, or her sisters'. Better to just smile and nod and then, maybe, she'd be left alone.

"You're right, of course," Willa said. Right now, if Mom said one plus one was five, she'd agree with her emphatically, just to get her off the phone.

"Make sure you send those e-mails at close."

"Okay. Talk to—"

Mom hung up and the dial tone responded instead of her mother's voice. Once upon a time, Willa had longed to hear the words "I love you" or "I'm proud of you" come out of Mom's mouth. Now, Willa knew better. Those words would never come. Her very existence insulted Mom somehow and Willa had resigned herself to accepting she'd never know why.

When she'd first called Mom to tell her of Aunt Jenny's disappearance, Mom's reaction surprised her. She hadn't expected Mom to support her decision to stay. Willa knew better than to think kind emotions drove her reaction, though. That woman already had her eye on a possible inheritance. In addition to stay-ing, Mom urged Willa to keep the shop open.

Willa questioned the advice at first. She didn't know how to run a bookstore, though she'd planned to learn. And surely the business shouldn't be a priority, especially not when the building could potentially be a crime scene.

The local police eliminated her latter concern, assuring her they'd scoured the little shop and found no signs of foul play. After a lengthy interrogation, they allowed her access to Bound to Please.

Despite knowing her mom wanted a piece of the profits, Willa agreed with her and kept the shop open in the hopes of uncovering the truth or something helpful for the investigation.

And, of course, she still hoped her aunt would return.

Mom was right on one account—with George out of the picture, Willa didn't have anything or anyone in Vancouver waiting for her return.

After finishing her morning routine, Willa flipped the sign over and opened the door to let some fresh air circulate through. She scrolled through her phone to find the right playlist. Today would be a classical day; the perfect music to soothe the lingering anger from her conversation with Mom.

Customers took advantage of the turn in the weather and trickled in to say hello. They all wanted to know how the investigation into Aunt Jenny's disappearance was going and more than a few purchased books—pity purchases, most likely, but if Aunt Jenny ever returned, Willa wanted to have some money waiting for her.

Willa put the duster behind the counter and tapped her fingers on the hard wood surface. She'd walked through every aisle this morning to dust the shelves, but her thoughts kept circling back to Lon and his stormy eyes, his strong hands, his hard body.

Her heart fluttered.

Business really was slow if all she did was stand here and lust after some random stranger. She'd already scoured social media, various online groups, and the websites of local insurance companies for more information.

Maybe she should sweep the floor. Again. She could take the books off the shelves one by one and clean behind them.

Willa needed to focus on how she might help find her missing aunt. Maybe she could do something, find something. Become the island's own Nancy Drew. Anything more than what she was currently doing.

The bell jingled as Alice Quinn walked through the front door. As the owner of a successful lodge at the end of Berry Point Road—one of the main streets on the island that ran along the coastline—Alice knew most of the residents. Her best friend, Georgia, operated the other bookstore on Gabe located in the island's "mall."

When Willa first met Alice two weeks ago, she'd expected some animosity or rivalry, but the older woman had been warm and welcoming. Motherly, if Willa had a good example to go by.

Alice nodded at the other customers as she made her way to Willa at the counter. "Ms. Murphy is under the weather today," she said, mentioning her neighbour who had a fruit farm down the road. "I'm looking for one of those old romance books she loves so much. Do you recommend anything?"

"Has she read the latest Scarlette LaFlamme?"

"Of course, she has," Alice replied with a laugh. "Do you have anything else?"

"I know just the thing." Willa smiled. "Follow me."

She stepped out from behind the counter and led Alice to the back corner of the store. The books in this section had covers that displayed half-naked, long-haired men in various lunge positions with distraught women throwing their bodice-wrapped curves against them. Willa had a hard time believing in fairy tale romances. Her only serious relationship certainly hadn't ended with a happily ever after, but Ms. Murphy loved these books.

"Perfect," Alice echoed her thoughts and then scanned through the used books. "You look a bit pensive, dear. What's on your mind?"

Willa hesitated. Lon's name rested on the tip of her tongue, but she swallowed it down. "Your family's been here for generations. Do you have any clue of Scarlette

LaFlamme's real identity?" The local celebrity of sorts wrote raunchy romantic smut and Willa kept running out of stock. No one knew the author's true identity, but the possibilities were boundless and enthusiastically debated.

Alice laughed and shook her head. "No, and if I knew, Ms. Murphy surely would've badgered it out of me by now. She's been on me for years for secrets I don't possess." She fingered the bindings of the old romance novels and walked a few steps away. "Are you sure it's LaFlamme you wanted to ask about?"

Willa glanced around to find them alone in the aisle. Well, with Ms. Murphy sick, no one else would be in this corner of the bookstore, anyway. "I need to get a hold of a customer from yesterday. But I only know his first name. I thought maybe, with your knowledge of everyone in town, you'd know how to reach him."

"It's a possibility. What's his name?"

"Lon."

She shook her head. "Odd name. Ms. Murphy has been around longer than me. She might know him. She's into everyone's business." Her tone turned a little sharp. Did Alice not appreciate Ms. Murphy being in *her* business?

Willa let the thought go and focused on Alice's suggestion. She had no intentions of grilling every local about a mysterious man. Maybe she'd have better luck if she knew more about Lon besides his first name.

Surely, others would've seen him if he'd been good friends with Aunt Jenny.

"Describe him for me." Alice pulled out a book and glanced at the cover before flipping it over.

A porcelain face carved by the ocean and eyes that contained a personal thunderstorm. Willa wrung her hands together as a wave of heat swept through her body. She couldn't say that. The woman would think her obsessed. She wanted to find out more about Lon because of his connection with her aunt. That was it. Totally, the only reason.

Alice turned to her expectantly.

Willa coughed into her fist. "Tall, strong, black hair, gray eyes. Do you know him?"

"Did he look like this, dear?" Alice held up a book with a dark-haired, bare-chested hero with a pirate ship run aground on the beach behind him. His chest and abs well-defined as if sculpted from rocks, chiseled cheekbones, a straight Greek nose, and piercing eyes that radiated heat from the worn cover.

"Yeah, that kind of nails it." She took a step away and reordered some of the books to hide her burning cheeks. "Minus the pirate ship, of course."

"Of course. But I don't think I know him." The older woman shook her head again and after reading the back cover of a few books, she waved one in the air. "This will do nicely."

They returned to the counter in silence.

"Is there anything else I can help you with?" Willa asked before ringing up Alice's purchase.

Alice looked up from staring at the old antique cash register. "No, dear. I'm sorry I don't know your Lon. I'm sure from your description I would remember him."

"He's not *my* Lon," she said, maybe a little too quickly. She fumbled to bag the woman's purchase.

The woman chuckled. "He must be something."

"He certainly left an impression." Willa handed Alice the bag without meeting her gaze.

Alice moved to the side so the large till didn't block her view and handed Willa the exact change for the book. "If I see your gentleman, I'll let him know you're looking for him."

"Thank you." Dang it. That was the last thing she wanted.

Alice flashed her a knowing smile before walking out of the store.

Willa placed the money in the till and slammed it shut. The change clanked around as the old register shook. Something fell inside.

Willa winced.

She shouldn't close the register so hard. The thing was ancient and probably irreplaceable. Jenny had found it in some pawn shop years ago. Willa still recalled the excitement in her aunt's voice when she told her all about it over the phone. "It's older than me," she'd said, like that was a good thing.

Willa shared her aunt's love for antiques. Mom, of course, had sneered when Willa mentioned the cash register in an attempt to make conversation. According to Mom, antique just meant old, and sellers used antique and vintage labels to fleece idiots who fell for trends.

Willa moved from behind the counter to help an older man with white hair and a slightly stooped posture with his purchase. He wanted a book for his granddaughter who'd moved to Saskatchewan with her family. Willa smiled and handed him Robert Munsch's *50 Below Zero.*

He chuckled and nodded.

While Willa rang up his purchase, she thought of her aunt. Why would she leave? Without a word, without money and without a struggle. Her aunt might be a recluse, but surely, she would've put up some sort of fight if someone forced her to leave.

Willa handed the man his purchase with a smile.

"That man," he leaned in and whispered. "The one you asked Alice about?"

Willa's body snapped to attention and her nails dug into the wood counter. "Yes?"

"I've seen him," he said. "Always down by the water."

That was vague. They lived on an island. Everything was near the water. "Which beach?"

He shrugged. "All of them at one time or another. Seems to like the water, that one."

The memory of his dripping black hair popped up in her mind. "Do you know him personally?"

"No," the man said, and then he leaned in. "Seems like the dangerous sort. I'd keep my distance if I were you." He held up the bag and nodded in thanks before sauntering out of the store, leaving Willa more torn than ever.

Willa pushed the cash register drawer to close it, but it stopped an inch short. She frowned, pulled the drawer out and slowly pushed it in again. It made a loud *thunk*, hitting something at the back. She pulled the drawer out, again, and leaned down. Nothing visible blocked the path of the drawer. She tried closing it again.

Well, of course it didn't work. Wasn't that the definition of stupidity? Doing the same thing over and over again and expecting different results? Or was that the definition of insanity?

She took a deep breath and pulled the drawer completely out. Extending her arm, she reached into the space and felt around. Her fingertips brushed something smooth and flat. She plucked the object and pulled it out.

Huh. A card.

She flipped it over and read the information. What the heck? Why did Aunt Jenny have Willa's birth certificate stashed at the back of her cash register? Willa ran her fingertips over the laminated card. The same size as a bank card, this was one of the older versions of the short form provincial birth certificate for Canada, or whatever they called it. With her full name, birthday, and location of birth, the card also had a bunch of numbers that meant nothing to her. Nowadays, they printed birth certificates on larger, indestructible plastic paper and included more information.

Willa flicked the card back and forth in her hand, reflecting the store lights from above. Surely this small card hadn't stopped the drawer from closing.

Willa shoved the card in her pocket and went fishing again, slowly moving her hand back and forth as she worked her way to the back of the space. Her fingertips slid over a round object. Cold and smooth, she gripped it and pulled her hand from the register. When she opened her hand, she found a smooth irregularly shaped rock resting on her palm. It was about an inch and a half in diameter, about half an inch in depth and looked like a river stone smoothed out from spending years under raging water. In the centre of the rock, there was a smooth hole. The edges of the hole weren't jagged, and the surface not cracked, so it must have been naturally made or very, very polished.

Huh.

What an odd rock. She dropped the stone in the cash register next to the toonies. Placing the drawer back, she slid the register shut. The drawer clicked in place. The rock must've been stashed somewhere inside the register, and she knocked it loose when she slammed the drawer.

Why would Aunt Jenny hide such a weird rock? But most importantly, why had Aunt Jenny stashed her birth certificate?

Like all her other questions, those too, remained unanswered.

CHAPTER
FIVE

"Life is jumping and elusive and momentously momentary."

— SANDY GINGRAS, *HOW TO LIVE AT THE BEACH*

After Willa closed the shop, she headed for Twin Beaches, the closest easily accessible beach to the store. Or rather...beaches. Unlike the cliff near the cylindrical pits off Eastham Road where sandstone was quarried for building construction and millstones for pulp and paper mills, Twin Beaches featured two bays one on each side of a road that lead to an isthmus. After checking Pilot Bay, the lesser used side of Twin Beaches, Willa headed toward the other one. Her boots sank into the flooded field as she tramped toward the waves of Taylor Bay.

Willa crested the small grassy ledge that led to the beach. A dog walker headed toward a road that accessed one side of the beach, but otherwise the area was empty. The tide had come almost all the way in, covering over one hundred meters of sand below its shallow depths. The strong smell of seaweed curled around her and a sudden urge to run into the gentle waves teased and pulled at her limbs.

No. Thrashing around in the frigid winter waters of British Columbia would be about as smart as standing at the edge of a cliff and not watching her footing.

Willa sighed and let the ocean air wash over her again. She'd always felt a pull to the ocean, but she lived in Vancouver—Burnaby—actually, and rarely came near it. When she did, she certainly didn't go in. Not in the Vancouver area with all the people, pollution, and litter. *No, thank you.*

Just standing here, inhaling the ocean air, had a calming effect, and she didn't have to share the moment with anyone. She should've made trips to the beach more of a priority, but the grind of everyday life sucked away her drive to do the very things she enjoyed. City life had a way of detaching the soul from nature.

Willa headed in the opposite direction of the dog walker, climbing the sandstone rocks lining the bay.

Barnacles crunched under her boots and light drizzle sprinkled her face. Slimy green algae covered some of the rocks. She'd learned from previous outings to avoid those slippery patches and still had the bruises on her arms and legs from the lessons.

As she walked, her mind raced. The ocean held no answers for her today, only more questions. Where exactly had Aunt Jenny disappeared to? Who was Lon? Why did Mom hate her so much when Willa tried so hard to please her?

The dark murky ocean had no answers. Instead, the sea foam floated by with abandoned chunks of seaweed, bits of crab shells and pine needles.

Did Aunt Jenny walk this way often? What would her aunt think about when she came this way? Willa closed her eyes and imagined Aunt Jenny standing beside her.

Short and petite with a lean body, her aunt would have her thick blonde hair pinned underneath a toque, but the long strands would dance in the gusts of ocean air. She'd be smiling, face flushed, blue eyes piercing, while she told Willa about the last book she read.

Willa's heart sunk. She crouched at the top of a large formation, cut from the sandstone by the waves over time. Purple starfish clung to the rocks below the surface and large fish swam by. Small boats anchored in the bay bobbed up and down with the gentle swells rolling toward the shoreline.

Her cell phone rang. Willa cringed. She didn't get

reception at the shop and most areas on the island, but apparently Mom could reach her here where she enjoyed the solitude. Maybe she'd just let it keep ringing.

Mom would keep calling.

She dug out the phone and accepted the call. "Hi, Mom."

"Where's the report?"

Willa cringed again. "I sold four books today. I didn't think a report was warranted."

"Four books? The shop will go under if you keep running it that way."

"It's the off season. Aunt Jenny told me she pretty much runs at a loss until the tourists start pouring in."

"Not good enough."

The wind whipped her hair across her face. She reached up with her free hand and pulled the strands back and tucked them behind her ear. "I don't know what you expect me to do."

"Better. I expect you to do better."

Willa sighed. Hadn't she spent her entire life trying to do exactly that?

"Honestly, sometimes I wonder why..." Mom bit off the rest of the sentence.

Something broke inside of her. The part that always held her back, the part that avoided conflict and let things slide. The wall simply crumbled. Willa refused to remain a wallflower. Not anymore. "Oh, don't stop there. You may as well get it out of your system," Willa said.

"I sometimes wonder how you could even be mine."

Willa had heard those hurtful words before, but for some reason, it didn't sound like that's what Mom originally intended to say.

"Sometimes I wonder the same thing." Willa hung up. She didn't need to hear Mom's screeching anymore. Done. She was done.

Mom hadn't always been that way, of course. While Willa remembered an echo of resentment and displeasure throughout her childhood, Mom hadn't truly voiced her disgust with Willa until Dad passed away ten years ago.

Grief slammed into her chest at his memory. She missed him, and so did Mom. Grief did a lot of things to people, but spontaneous hatred for one's own daughter didn't seem like a normal response. Yet, for the longest time, Willa rationalized Mom's behaviour, mentally defending her and trying to find empathy and reason instead of a backbone.

As the years went on, though, Mom's obvious disdain for her youngest daughter grew stronger and made less and less sense. Willa hadn't caused the cancer in Dad's pancreas.

Instead of ending her walk feeling invigorated, Willa shuffled back to the shop with an empty heart and a stomach twisted into a knot.

CHAPTER
SIX

"We want to [stretch] the days, distill the memories, make them last."

— SANDY GINGRAS, *HOW TO LIVE
AT THE BEACH*

THIRTY YEARS AGO...

Skye waited in the secret cavern. She waited like she did every day for the last two weeks. The torrential downpour outside sent streams of rainwater down the cracks and holes in the ceiling. Her teeth chattered from the cold as she hugged herself and tried to stay warm and stop the shaking.

Where was he?

Why wasn't he here?

She had important news to share, and she didn't know what to do.

The wind outside howled and the numbing water at her feet slapped the sloped ground angrily. She'd have to leave soon.

Instead of slipping back into the ice-cold water, her feet remained glued to the sandstone. If she left, she'd have to accept what his absence meant. Before coming here today, she'd made a promise to herself that this was the last time, his last chance.

The wind roared outside. The trees groaned, shaking the cave. Another twenty minutes passed.

Skye gulped.

Fine, then. She could take a hint.

She turned to leave, her hand slipping to her flat stomach. She'd have to do this alone, and that scared her the most.

CHAPTER
SEVEN

"We know that the beauty is in the evanescence."

— SANDY GINGRAS, *HOW TO LIVE
AT THE BEACH*

CURRENT DAY...

"I hear you've been looking for me." A deep voice spoke behind Willa.

She jumped in her seat to find Lon standing behind her at the local café. "Lon? You startled me."

"Sorry about that." He wore nicer clothes than the last time they met, but rain still dripped from the ends of his hair. "Are you okay? Your head took some good hits the other day."

"I'm fine. I have a history of banging myself up, so

I've done worse. Did you get caught out in the storm again?" She glanced outside at the gray skies. The rain fell so hard it bounced off the pavement in the parking lot. Thunder rocked the coffee shop and lighting streaked through the air.

"I certainly did." He smiled, a small smile, like he thought of something funny, and she suddenly wished she knew the inside joke.

A number of other patrons had turned toward or glanced over at Lon, taking in his dishevelled appearance. For some reason, she found that comforting. Like, it confirmed she hadn't imagined Lon's existence.

"Who told you I was looking for you?" she asked.

"Some old guy I see around the marina now and then." His gaze flicked to the chair across from her. "May I join you?"

"Of course." She straightened in her seat. "How'd you know to find me here?"

He chuckled and held up his coffee in a takeaway cup. "I didn't. I planned to caffeinate first and then head over to the bookstore. You know, make a better impression than before." He slid into the leather chair across from her, his knees bumping into hers.

"Sorry." She sat back in her seat.

"Sorry," he said at the same time, running his hand through his wet locks. "I'm the one who bumped you."

She waved off his apology and flashed him a smile. "So, how's work? This recent weather must be good for business."

His lips twitched. "Jenny always said it isn't work if you're having fun."

Memories of Aunt Jenny saying the same thing to her sent fuzzy warmth through her body. She raised her cup and drank some latte. "And are you?"

"Having fun?" His gaze flashed. "I am now."

She chuckled. "Flirt."

"Can you blame me?"

"No, but I can question your taste."

He leaned forward, bringing his scent with him— sea salt and fresh air. He reminded her of long walks on the beach in winter with the salt spray spritzing her skin, which was completely ridiculous.

If George heard her internal thoughts, he'd ridicule her and accuse her of drifting off to dream land. Her ex was all about practicality, logic and making connections that provided him with something or helped propel him further in his career.

Willa mentally shook herself.

Well, George wasn't here, and she needed to stop thinking about him and what he wanted or what he'd think. He never afforded her the same courtesy when they were together. And frankly, she never should've dated him in the first place.

"How's the book business?" Lon asked.

"Slow."

He lifted his takeaway cup and drank. "Jenny always said the winter months nearly broke her. She was in the process of setting up an online store to help mitigate the low numbers during the off season."

Willa perked up. Aunt Jenny had mentioned something she needed help with. Maybe the online store was that thing. Willa didn't have a lot of skills, but online shopping was definitely one of them.

"You look like a cat that got the cream." Lon's smile nearly blinded her.

"You just answered how I can help my aunt until she returns."

His gaze shuttered and he placed his cup on the table. "Do you think she'll come back?"

Her stomach twisted from all the dark thoughts she refused to entertain. She watched a lot of crime dramas. Like, a lot. She knew the first twenty-four hours were the most critical and yet they had no more insight into Aunt Jenny's disappearance now than they had when they first realized she'd gone missing.

"I don't know," she whispered. "But I have to hope."

Lon reached out and placed his hand over hers. That weird tingling sensation spread along her skin from the contact. "It will be okay."

"Surely we would've heard something from her by now if that were the case." She eyed her half-finished latte, no longer feeling thirsty or in need of caffeine.

Lon squeezed her hand before letting go. "I take it they haven't found anything new?"

Did he seek her out to gather more information?

She understood the fascination. More than a few locals came by the store regularly to fish for new gossip. She didn't make a fuss about it, though, because they usually purchased something while trying to dig.

"I assume they haven't," she answered honestly. "They wouldn't tell me anyway, not with it being an open investigation."

He nodded and drank more coffee. "I wish there was something. Missing items or something out of the ordinary. Some clue as to what happened."

She sighed and pushed her cup to the side. "Apparently, she had a yellow raincoat, and I haven't found that among her things. I also haven't found any gumboots. For someone living on the west coast, I'd expect at least one pair. I have several."

He pressed his lips together. "So, she went out with a yellow raincoat and gumboots?"

"Complete conjecture."

"Not really. Jenny loved to go for walks, and I know the raincoat you're referring to. She had dark gumboots. Navy blue if I recall correctly."

Willa sat up in her chair. "Well, that's something, I suppose."

He flashed her a small smile. "I wish there was more."

"Me too. The only other thing out of the ordinary is my birth certificate." For some reason, she didn't want to mention the weird rock with the hole in it.

"I'm not following." He frowned, his dark

eyebrows slashing down. "Why would your birth certificate be out of the ordinary?"

She shrugged. "It might not be. I found a copy of my birth certificate in Aunt Jenny's register. Maybe she found it with some of my father's things when she helped settle the estate. It just seems odd she never mentioned it."

Lon grunted, non-committal, and drank more coffee. How did he take his coffee? Was it as black as his hair, or did he put enough cream in it to make it beige?

"I highly doubt my birth certificate is related to my aunt's disappearance, though."

Lon put his cup down on the table again and nodded solemnly. "Probably not."

They sat in silence, Lon drinking coffee and Willa staring at hers hoping some magical answer would pop out of its creamy depths. Caffeine was the answer to a lot of things but solving a missing person's case was not one of them.

"Tell me about your life in Van." Lon broke the silence.

"Not much to tell." She shrugged and glanced outside. The rain showed no signs of letting up. She'd have to brave the downpour to get back to the store. Customers were unlikely to show up today, so hopefully she'd get a good start on the online store. She needed to find a platform, register a domain, and start figuring out a way to integrate their inventory with an online catalogue. "I should head back."

"Ready to start on the online store?" Lon asked.

"Am I that obvious?"

"I can see the wheels turning in that head of yours from here." He played with the takeaway cup on the table. "I'm not very good with computers, but I am familiar with your aunt's catalogue and inventory system. Would you like some help?"

"I'd love it."

CHAPTER
EIGHT

"Every wave comes in, then retreats."

— SANDY GINGRAS, *HOW TO LIVE
AT THE BEACH*

A loud crash of thunder rocked the old house and stirred up the scents from the late winter morning. A streak of lightning followed an instant later, flashing white and orange across Willa's vision as though she lay directly under the storm, instead of her bedroom's ceiling.

Another loud boom rattled the furniture.

The wind howled through the tree branches and rain pounded the rooftops and road outside. In the distance, the eerie low sound of a foghorn moaned.

Willa cast her bedding aside. She couldn't sleep. She kept thinking of her missing aunt and Lon. He'd sat with her in the store for hours, helping her figure out a way to make her computer program for the store's inventory speak to the online program for virtual shoppers. He had been honest when he said he knew little about computers, but he was great at working through problems. After they called it a night, they'd drank tea in the kitchen and Willa shared stories of her misadventures as a child. It wasn't until he left that she realized she learned nothing more about him or his relationship with Aunt Jenny.

That was two days ago, and she hadn't seen Lon since. She still didn't know his full name, where he lived, where he was from or how to reach him. All she knew was how he made her feel and that was dangerous information all on its own.

Willa padded down the stairs, flicked on the lights and turned on the kettle. Maybe she had a masochistic streak, wanting to drink more of the tea she shared with Lon. Once she plopped the tea bag in her cup—a sacrilegious tea method according to Mom—she sat down and inhaled the bevy of herbal scents. The steam lifted off the tea and warmed her face, and the tension eased from her shoulders.

She'd closed the shop a bit early and spent some time cleaning up the backyard. The destructive storm from earlier had ravaged the trees and Willa had spent hours clearing branches and raking leaves. With the wind howling outside again, she probably should've just let it be.

She wished there was more she could do for the sad-looking trees. They stood so tall and regal, defying the dry summer heat and cold winters. She found herself talking to them like an idiot, as if they were people, not bark and sap. Now they were probably getting another good thrashing, littering the ground with more branches, twigs, and needles.

Thump! Thump! Thump!

She gasped. It couldn't be.

Thump! Thump! Thump!

She clutched her hot mug in both hands and turned toward the doorway leading to the bookstore. From the kitchen in the back room, she had a clear view through the store to the front door, but not who stood on the other side.

"Willa!" Lon growled from the other side of the door. "Please wake up and let me in!"

Willa gasped and almost dropped the cup. The tea sloshed around, and some spilled over her hands. It burned, but she didn't move. She couldn't breathe. Somehow the air got trapped in her throat. Why was he here?

She bit her lip. Maybe he had news about Aunt Jenny. Maybe he wasn't as intimidating or devastating to look at as she remembered.

She set the cup down on the table and scrambled to the bookstore's front door.

Thump! Thump! Thump!

"Willa! It's raining!" Lon yelled.

"Shush," she hissed back. "I'm coming." She flicked on the lights, unbolted the door and swung it open.

Lon stood with his arms at his sides, pelted by the rain. His hair lay plastered to his face and his storm gray eyes burned with each lightning flash.

Willa's breath caught in her throat, and she pressed her fingertips into the cold metal of the doorknob.

"Hi," Lon said.

"Hi," she replied.

The rain splattered his body and face as she studied his strong frame. Lon cleared his throat. "May I come in?"

Willa folded her arms across her chest. "Tell me your full name."

His lips twitched. His smile quickly turned to a grimace as the storm renewed its attack. "Lon Devlin."

"Middle name?"

"Storm." He flinched at the hail battering the side of his cheek and shook his head. "Hippy parents."

"Huh." She continued to study him, or more accurately, his torso, and the way his shirt clung to his broad chest. His clothes were nicer tonight, or at least had been before the rain got to them. He wore a gray polo shirt, dark form-fitting jeans, white-washed with strategically placed rips for fashion, and designer runners.

"Willa?" Lon's voice rumbled with the thunder.

She jumped and her face warmed. "Oh, sure.

Here. Please come in." She moved back and made a large sweeping gesture for him to follow.

Lon brushed passed her, carrying the fresh smell of the sea in his wake. She shut the door with both hands and took a long breath before turning around.

"How are you?" Lon walked ahead and then pivoted to study her from the center of the bookstore. "How's the online set-up going?"

"It's fine. I've run into a little bit of a snag, but I think I'll be able to work it out." She smoothed errant hair out of her face with a shaky hand. She needed to get information out of this man.

Lon continued to stare at her as if the sheer force of his gaze would bring forth some unknown truth from the depths of her soul.

Willa glared back. While she attempted to exude defiance on the outside, her insides quelled at such an antic. George would never have stood for it. And her mother... No, there was no defying Mother. That woman's tongue proved more dangerous than the wooden spoon she used to pummel Willa's butt with when she misbehaved as a child.

The tension on Lon's face eased into a smile. "We need to talk."

"What kind of weather insurance salesman wanders around in the middle of the night, without proper clothes or a car?" She'd crossed her arms again and quickly dropped them to her sides.

"I never said I was good at it." He nodded toward

the back of the bookstore. "Look, can we sit down and talk?"

Neither of them moved.

"I'm not sure what good that will do," she said. Why was she suddenly annoyed? It wasn't his fault she'd let his good looks distract her into talking about herself instead of gleaning information from him.

"Why's that?" He raised an eyebrow.

"Well, I don't know anything, and neither, apparently, do you, so we're just going to talk around each other and be no closer to finding my aunt than before."

Lon pursed his lips. "I see the problem."

"What do you want?" she asked. "And please don't try to tell me you came here in the middle of the night to help me with my online store."

Lon tilted his head and paused, as if hearing something in the wind besides the storm howling. "I want to know what happened to Jenny. She's a dear friend, and I'd never wish harm to come to her."

The tension eased from Willa's shoulders, and she studied the strong man in front of her. He could have barged in at any time and harmed her, but he hadn't. He could've stolen whatever he wanted the last two times he was here but hadn't. He could've lied to her about everything, but minus the salesman line...he hadn't.

"Is that all?" she asked, barely whispering the question.

His gaze flashed. "No, I want a lot more than that.

But I'll settle for great company and searching for clues to solve the mystery around Jenny's disappearance."

She bit her lip and then nodded. "I want to find out what happened to Jenny, too."

"What do you suggest?"

Willa opened her mouth and then shut it. She wasn't asked for her opinion often, not since Dad died. She used to have friends, great friends, but lost touch after years of devoting her time and energy to her relationship with George. When they broke up, she realized she had nothing, and no one left of her own. Her current "friends" had only really been acquaintances or the wives of George's friends. Only one of her original pre-George friends had stuck it out over the years and after George left Willa, the reason why became abundantly clear.

"Willa? Do you have any ideas?"

"I...uh..."

Lon tilted his head again and took a couple of steps toward her. "You're a smart woman. I'm sure you don't intend to just sit in this store and do nothing forever. What do you plan to do?"

"I was going to search Aunt Jenny's study," she admitted. After she fixed the glitch with the online store, searching the house for more clues was on the top of her list.

"You haven't already?"

His tone held no accusation, only surprise, but it still cut. Willa's head snapped up. "I haven't had time. I only got here two weeks ago and while I planned to help Jenny, I hadn't prepared for running a bookstore on my own with no help. I spent the first few days in denial and expected my aunt to walk through the door at any moment. Then I filed a missing person's report and spent a couple of days at the lodge while the police searched this building, questioned me and confirmed my timeline of events. They also searched the store and had it closed off as a potential crime scene for a bit. Since then, I've been getting my feet under me with the bookstore. And now there's the online store stuff."

Lon held his hands up in surrender. "Willa, it's okay. I'm just surprised, is all. Did the police come up with anything from their search?"

"Not that I know of, but they made a mess of the place. I've spent more time cleaning and doing inventory than anything else."

"I thought Jenny had a large family. Why aren't more of them here helping out?"

"They all have lives," she mumbled. Like she needed or wanted a reminder of that fact.

"What?" he asked.

Oops. She hadn't meant to speak out loud, but whenever she thought of her family, that familiar anger boiled up from her core. She lifted her chin and met his gaze. "According to my mom, I'm a complete failure as a daughter and woman. My fiancé left me, so I'm unmarried and childless at thirty. Well, almost thirty. My sisters all have families, and their time is apparently more valuable, as is my mom's, because they have things to do."

Despite snapping the words at Lon, she wanted him to know the truth. His mere presence seemed to draw it out of her.

His eyes widened at first, but then a deep rumble filled the room, as if the storm had moved inside. Lon stood with his feet planted shoulder width apart, muscles tense, fists clenched. The air stirred and whirled in a mini tornado around him, flashing blue and silver.

No, that's not right.

No one had eyes like that. She squinted and leaned forward. The air didn't move in streams, nor did it flash colours. Lon certainly didn't emit rumbling sounds like thunder.

Maybe she had suffered a concussion. She really should go to see a doctor if she kept seeing things.

Lon took a slow breath in and smiled at her. It was the first time since they'd met, that his flash of pearly whites came across as insincere. He shimmied his shoulders a little and took the final steps forward to reach her. His hand slowly rose to gently take her own.

Despite his skin being chilled from the weather outside, warmth flooded her body from the contact.

"Forget about your family. No offense, but they sound like idiots. Let's go see what we can find," he said and gave her a little tug.

She nodded, not wanting him to let her hand go,

but he did, and they headed for Aunt Jenny's study. The stairs groaned under their weight.

"I have to warn you," Willa said as they reached the second floor and turned the corner to the hallway. "It's quite a mess."

Lon shrugged and swept his arm out for her to lead.

They reached the spare room Aunt Jenny used as a study, and Willa pushed the door open.

He followed and then lurched to a stop. "Wow."

She hadn't been kidding. Jenny's study looked like the storm outside had raged for days in the large space, minus the rain and hail. Papers, books, and upturned boxes littered the floor. Jenny referred to her personal library as the study and though they seldom video chatted, when they did, Aunt Jenny always had a wide smile on her face when she mentioned this room. Aunt Jenny loved books and spent the majority of her time with her nose stuck in one.

"I warned you." Willa ran her hand through her blonde hair and winced when her fingers brushed the bump on the back of her head.

He nodded and took a deep breath to survey the room again. "Did the police do this?"

"Before they searched the house, the place had been immaculate. Pretty surprising. My aunt's known to drift to the flaky side when it comes to organization. She must've cleaned up right before she vanished." *For me.* Willa's stomach clenched.

"Anything missing?" Lon asked.

Willa rolled her eyes.

Despite her response, Lon smiled. "Did I ask that already?"

"Honestly? I don't know. I've heard the question so often that I'm not sure who's asked and who hasn't. Aside from the yellow raincoat and boots, I'm not aware of anything missing, but it's not like I had an itemized list of my aunt's possessions before I arrived."

"Fair enough. Where shall we start?" He brushed his hands on his jeans and nudged a box out of the way with his foot.

She hesitated. Lon looked to her to take the lead instead of ordering her around. He was respectful and courteous. Nice. His smile tugged at Willa's heart and made her feel things and she hated herself for it. Being nice shouldn't be a grand accomplishment, it should be the bare fucking minimum. Yet, pair that with his black-as-night hair and mesmerizing gaze and Willa found it hard to come up with reasons to stay away from her guest.

"Let's sort through paperwork," she said. Oh look, she could still speak. "Business and personal. Since there's not much in the way of bookstore crime, if anything bad happened to my aunt, I'm guessing it was personal."

"Smart."

She could get used to having Lon around. She liked how he made her feel safe and comfortable.

Secure. The heat in his gaze made her feel attractive and wanted.

Willa cringed from her thoughts, again. Wasn't she just sad? Her expectations for other human beings had dropped so low.

She turned a box over and started rifling through the paper. All business invoices. While she worked, Lon knelt down and neatly piled the papers together. His forearm muscles contracted and relaxed with each simple movement and transfixed her.

Willa peeled her gaze away from him and moved to the opposite corner of the room. She opened another box and started scanning more papers.

"So, you were engaged?" he asked, his voice more gravelly than usual.

Though she faced away, her whole body tensed, and her hands froze on a piece of paper.

"Sorry. Probably not the best conversation starter, but I'd like to hear the story if you're willing to share it."

"Don't apologize." She shrugged. "He left me for my best friend. There's nothing more to tell."

"I disagree. Obviously, the man is an idiot. What happened?"

Willa sighed and finally turned to face him, knowing her pained expression probably gave away everything. "I don't know. I did everything he wanted, the way he wanted, and it still wasn't enough."

It was never enough. Not for George. Not for Mom or her sisters. Not for anyone.

The paper crinkled in Lon's fist. He took a deep breath before speaking. "Maybe that was the problem."

"You think it's my fault, too?" Ugh. Maybe she should just kick him out now. She didn't need anyone to help her feel like crap. She did well enough at that on her own.

"Not at all. But you can't go through life doing what others want. When was the last time you did something for yourself?" he asked.

She paused and ran her hand through her hair again.

"And don't tell me when you got your hair or nails done, that doesn't count," he added.

Dammit. That was exactly what she'd planned to say.

"When was the last time you did something, anything, just for you?"

"I...I don't know." She bit her lip. "Coming here to work and live with my aunt is probably the closest thing to what you're asking."

"That's not right."

Great. Another person judging her. Judging and finding her lacking. Why couldn't she find someone who liked her for who she was? She clenched her fists and stalked toward him. "Don't you dare."

"What?" He dropped the papers from his hands.

"Don't you dare judge me." She crumpled the

paper in her hand to jab her finger into his chest. "You don't even know me." Not really. She barely recognized herself some days.

"You're right." He grabbed both her balled fists and held them to his body. "But I want to."

Willa froze as he bent his head closer.

"I want to know all of you," he said.

Lon's words coursed through Willa's body, awakening a deep need. The anger riding her earlier washed away as a tsunami of desire rolled through her. She felt weak and strong at the same time, and she wanted nothing more than to rip her hands from his grasp and yank his face to hers.

His eyes churned with an inner storm; swirls of gray, dark blue and swamp green surrounded dilated pupils. Nobody could have eyes like that, could they? He seemed to see right to the marrow of her bones, as if he really saw her, as if he knew her already, despite being an almost complete stranger.

A stranger.

She didn't know this man.

She couldn't make out with a hot stranger. Her aunt was missing for goodness sake. How could she even entertain the thought? She shook her head and pushed away. He released her hands automatically, but his eyebrows pinched together, giving him a severe otherworldly expression despite his softening eyes. She took a step back, but he remained where he was, a solid temptation only a foot away. She'd give anything to feel his hands on her right now, experience that tingling sensation his skin made when it touched hers. Chemistry. That's what it was. They had physical chemistry. She'd never felt anything like it before.

"I...we...we can't." She wrapped her arms around her chest.

"Can't what?" He frowned.

"Can't...Oh, never mind." Heat spread through her face. She turned around and picked up some papers with shaky hands. She'd almost made a fool of herself. Worse, her body still vibrated with need. Her eyes struggled to focus on the paper.

Invoices. More invoices.

"Willa," Lon said.

She squeezed her eyes shut and tried not to imagine how his lips would burn against her own. He shuffled his feet somewhere behind her, but she couldn't turn to meet his gaze. He'd read her feelings like Aunt Jenny read books. She shook her head and bent to put the business items in an open box.

"Willa." Lon spoke again, imploring.

She sighed and turned around.

Lon stood exactly as he had before, as if only his mouth had moved. His hands still hung at his sides, his palms toward her in an unthreatening gesture, as if beckoning her to return to him. He flinched when her gaze met his.

"What?" she asked.

"We were only talking," he said.

"Yeah, sure," She brushed a clump of hair out of her face. This was infinitely worse. She'd misread the moment. Here she was making a big deal about something that wasn't even going to happen. Story of her life. Thankfully, she hadn't tried to kiss him. That would've been even more embarrassing.

"But," Lon continued. "We could do more."

"What's that supposed to mean?" She flipped an overturned banker's box right side up and retrieved a slip of paper that had fallen out.

"You said we can't as if there was a law written somewhere." He paused and took a deep breath. "But if you want something to happen, there's no reason why it couldn't."

Willa froze, half bent with the paper in her hand, heart hammering in her chest. She didn't know what to say. What could she say? Maybe she hadn't misread anything after all. He looked at her like he wanted to devour her.

"It means," Lon continued, taking a step forward. "There are no moms, sisters, or ignorant ex fiancés here to judge you or get in our way. You're a grown woman, Willa. You make your own choices. And just to be perfectly clear, Jenny has only ever been a friend. We were never involved romantically."

She dropped the paper in her hand and straightened. When she met the intensity in Lon's face, she almost looked away again, but something about his expression, the way his body angled forward, his brows pinched in, his eyes blazed—something about him dared her not to. She squared her shoulders and stared back.

"It's up to you," he said.

"Up to me?" she repeated, unsure of the words. "Pretty sure it takes two to tango."

His smile widened and he leaned forward. "I want nothing more than to kiss you until you beg me to throw you on that pile of books and show you what a real man can do. But I'm not doing a damn thing unless you want me to. You make the move, Willa. You decide." He put his hands on his hips and waited.

The air sucked out of Willa's lungs. Her heartbeat thudded in her ears and her palms started to sweat. He wanted to kiss her. Her body ached for his touch but her stupid brain, her stupid, stupid brain wouldn't stop parroting that she shouldn't be doing this, that she couldn't be.

"I think we should find out what happened to my aunt," she said, wincing even as the words came out of her mouth.

Seriously? She found it difficult to like herself on a regular basis, she didn't need add any additional reasons.

Lon smiled and his body almost vibrated with energy, as if he gained some unseen power or insight. "Then let's keep looking."

She nodded and went back to sorting—bills, bills, bills, bank statement, bank statement, bills. All the while, she sensed Lon's body moving around the room, as if her own was hyper-aware of his. "Do you have any family?"

"A bunch of brothers." Lon's deep rumbling voice broke the tension in the room.

She glanced at him, not daring to meet his powerful gaze. "How many?"

"Sometimes it feels like they make up an entire horde," he said.

"Are they like you?" she asked, not quite sure exactly what she meant.

"Physically, we're almost all identical, which as you can imagine led to a lot of fun and trouble at the same time. Mentally...Well, we have a lot of similar views, but not always. We've grown apart more recently, and I don't see them often."

"I'm sorry."

He shrugged. "It happens. These things are cyclical. I'm sure I will spend more time with them soon enough, and then I'll lament the days I had peace and quiet without them in my life."

She snorted. "How did you meet Jenny?"

"Ah, well." He looked away, pink tinging his cheeks. "That's an embarrassing story."

She put down the stack of bills and straightened. "Which means you must tell me right now."

He sighed and looked at the ceiling, perhaps for divine intervention. When nothing happened, he turned to her, his lips tugging up at one corner. "She found me stranded on the beach during one of her morning walks. I wasn't in the greatest shape. She clothed me, fed me, and kept me company while I recovered from a traumatizing experience. I returned later to thank her for her kindness and friendship bloomed."

"What happened?"

His expression shuttered. "I'd rather not say."

Every cell in her body itched to ask more. She bit her lip and looked away. If he didn't want to share that story with her, he didn't have to.

He cleared his throat. "Why don't you tell me more about your overbearing mom and ass of an ex?"

"How did you—"

"Know your ex was an ass?" he finished for her. "He voluntarily left you. That's obvious. And he was a cheater."

"No, not George. How'd you know my mom was overbearing?"

"I'm Jenny's friend, remember? She told me about her sister-in-law and crazy nieces."

"Oh!"

"She never mentioned you, though. Never talked about you. I wonder why."

"Oh." Willa's heart stopped thudding in her chest and sank a little. Of all her family members, Willa had been the closest to her aunt. Before he died, her father used to call them two peas in a pod. Why wouldn't Aunt Jenny talk about her?

"Willa, I'm sure she had her reasons. She didn't speak often about your family, and when she did, her voice filled with anger and hurt all at the same time. She only let a few things slip. I suspected there was more to the story." His gaze softened. "She must've kept you separate in her words and her heart from the rest of your clan."

Willa nodded and tried to ignore the sting in her eyes. Her gaze caught on the paper she dropped and stooped to pick it up. With a flick of her wrist, she flipped the paper over. What the hell?

"What is it?" Lon asked.

"Adoption papers."

"For whom?"

She scanned the paper and froze. Numbness spread through her body. The writing stared back at her, taunting. A name so familiar, she'd recognize it anywhere. "For me."

CHAPTER
NINE

"Every day promises, then turns its back and slips away."

— SANDY GINGRAS, *HOW TO LIVE AT THE BEACH*

Lon walked over and plucked the paper from Willa's hands. His eyebrows rose as his gaze studied the adoption certificate. "Your adoption?"

"Why would Aunt Jenny have this? Why would no one tell me?" Had Aunt Jenny discovered Mom and Dad adopted her and planned to tell her? "It makes sense now."

"What does?" Lon frowned. "Because where I'm standing nothing makes sense."

She shook her head. "My mom's animosity. Her hatred toward me. I'm not her daughter."

"If she hated you so much, why hasn't she told you?"

Willa shrugged. "Maybe she promised Dad before he passed away. She might not care for me, but she loved Dad. Mourning him is pretty much the only thing we have ever had in common." Another memory percolated. "Maybe my mom tried to tell me, in her own way, giving me hints without breaking her promise. She's always saying how I'm so different from her."

"The identity of your biological parents isn't listed."

Willa frowned. "Maybe my mom knows."

"Do you think she'll tell you?" He sounded as skeptical as she felt.

"If she hasn't by now, probably not." An idea struck her, an awful yet oddly delightful thought. "I look like my dad and aunt."

Lon paused. "What are you saying?"

"Maybe I'm the result of an affair." Why did Dad's possible infidelity make her feel better? God, she was an awful person.

"That would definitely explain why your mom hates you."

She bobbed her head. "A constant reminder of Dad's infidelity. I can almost understand." Almost.

"Yet, you were a child. The sins of the parents shouldn't be paid for by their children."

"Yet here I am."

"Here you are." His gaze flashed. "Are you going to confront your mom?"

"Absolutely."

His smile spread. "Why don't you tell me about your family some more? Last time we spoke, you told me all about your childhood and your dad. What about your mom and sisters?"

"Why would you want to know about them?"

"I want to know all about you, Willa."

At first Willa hesitated to open up, but after a few deep breaths and a few words, she vented with passion. She told Lon about her sisters and their cruel jokes. She even mentioned Dad and a sweet memory she hadn't thought of in years. With each word, the tension in her body eased. As her story about the last time she took Dad out for coffee and he tried to set her up with the barista came to an end, she felt like a weight had been lifted off her shoulders. She flashed Lon a smile and reached for another box.

Lon laughed and shook his head. "Your father sounds like quite the character."

"He is. Was."

"You must miss him a lot," he said.

"I do." She looked down at her feet, not wanting to make eye contact.

"Thank you for sharing that story with me," he said.

She wanted to share more. She also wanted to touch him, to feel his skin on hers and no amount of talking had eased the ache.

They'd sorted most of the paperwork and had only the books left. The pages probably didn't contain the answers to Jenny's disappearance, but they kept working anyway. She didn't want this night to end, and from the way Lon's determined brows furrowed as she continued to talk, he didn't want to stop either.

A thought struck her. A devious thought.

He'd said no one was here to judge her. He'd said he wanted to kiss her. If she didn't want the night to end, it didn't have to.

She put down the stack of papers she held and studied the man across the room from her. He listened to her, valued her opinion and gave her choices. He made her feel safe and empowered. He could easily demand, intimidate or manipulate, but he seduced with the sheer intensity of his gaze and the kindness in his heart.

Lon looked up and caught her looking. "What is it?"

"You were right." She walked over to him on borrowed confidence. The room wasn't that big, so it didn't take long.

"Of course." He ducked his head down a bit. "But just so we're clear, what was I right about?"

"There's no one else in this room but us, and we're two consenting adults."

Before she could talk herself out of it, before she let logic reveal all the reasons why this was a bad idea, she reached up, clutched his head by his hair and dragged his mouth down to hers.

His lips felt so good. Like she'd imagined, like she'd dreamt about—full and soft, yet firm and wicked. His arms closed around her, pulling her into the strength of his body. When he sucked her bottom lip, a shiver of pleasure radiated from her core. His tongue slipped into her mouth and caressed her own.

She'd never experienced such an explosive kiss. She gripped him harder, her mouth opening wider to taste more, and his tongue answered back.

His hands slid down her back to clutch her butt and he pressed his groin against hers. His erection dug into her. She wanted to rip his pants off and feel the smoothness of his skin. To hell with her mom. Her sisters. George. To hell with them all. She never got what she wanted, and she'd be damned if she'd miss out on this.

His hands never stopped moving, caressing her back, running down her sides, brushing her breasts, before gripping her hips. Waves of heat coursed through her body at his touch.

She'd never lusted after a man like this before, never wanted something so physical. Yet, the moment she stared into those storm-gray eyes, she could think of nothing else, no one else. She'd felt lost when he disappeared like some sort of magical fairy. Her thoughts were silly, of course. He was just a man. Just a man that she wanted inside her right now.

Lon slid his hands up her shirt, his fingers smooth icicles against her skin. She jerked, and then relaxed as the coolness soaked into her body like trickles of rain.

Her skin ached for more, and when he slipped her shirt off, only momentarily breaking contact from her lips, she knew she'd get it. Heat burned through her body.

Every point of contact between her skin and his vibrated with energy, sending searing tingles up her limbs and through her body. She couldn't get enough. She moved her hands down to grasp his waistband and glanced behind her. Nowhere comfortable to go, no bed handy, but who cared? There was a clear spot on the floor a few steps away.

She tugged on his jeans and pulled him in that direction. Lon chuckled against her mouth, then he trailed kisses down her neck to her collarbone. He placed his hands on her hips again and let her guide him. He'd probably let her do whatever she wanted.

Willa's head tipped back, and a soft moan escaped her lips as Lon's mouth moved to her breast. She stepped back again, now determined to feel all this man had to offer, take whatever he gave. Her heel caught on something, and she staggered. With her weight unbalanced, she groped to grab onto something, but there was only Lon. She clutched at his damp shirt. Lon jerked back, but it was too late.

They toppled over in a heavy heap.

Her back slammed against the hardwood panels.

Lon somehow snaked an arm underneath to break some of her fall. Her head barely tapped the ground, but an instant throb started at the base of her skull. Lon's other arm braced on the floor while he dipped his head between her breasts and breathed deeply; in and out, in and out. His forearm must be killing him.

Then his body started to shake. His shoulders trembled, and his breathing hitched. How badly did he hurt himself? Then she heard it, a deep rumble over the thunder outside.

He was laughing.

Lon pressed his forehead pressed against her breast and chuckled. "I hoped to be a bit more graceful. Are you okay?"

"I'm fine." Willa squirmed a bit under his hold. "And that was my fault. I tripped on something."

"Do you make a habit of flailing around?"

"Only since I met you," she lied. She pushed up and he scrambled to get out of the way so she could sit up.

They studied one another before breaking into silly grins.

"It was that book." Willa pointed to the massive tome at his feet.

"Stupid book," he said. He bent down to pick up

the book but snatched his hand back at the last minute and hissed.

She frowned at him and knelt to scoop the book into her hands. Her palms tingled on the leather binding as she lifted it onto her lap. "Look at this thing. It's ancient."

Lon didn't reply, but the book held her fascination. She used her shirt sleeve to brush off the dust and then read out the title. "The Encyclopedia of Mythical Creatures."

Her voice echoed in the room as she flipped open the heavy cover and gently leafed through the pages. A small dust cloud floated up from the pages. Bookmarks and sticky notes stuck out from the paper edges.

Willa reached up and thumped Lon's arm. "She marked a few pages."

"Yeah?" he asked, his voice sounding a little empty.

Willa flipped to a scene with an artist's depiction of the ocean with white, blue, and gray wisps playing in the curve of a wave.

"This one's got your name on it." Willa beamed up at him. "She must've wanted to show it to you."

Lon pursed his lips before returning her smile. He seemed a little stiff. Maybe he didn't enjoy massive books with magical creatures.

"Look at the artwork." She leaned back so he could see the picture and read the information on the opposite page. "Tempest. A water sprite who can only take human form during storms. Ruled by the God of the

Oceans, water sprites are potent flows of energy vaguely taking human shape under water. They ride the tides, waves, and undertows of the ocean and feed off the energy from the movement of water. Although they do the bidding of their sea god, they are relatively harmless unless defending their god or the knowledge of their..." She gulped. "...existence. They have been known to drown fair maidens to delight in their beauty..." Her voice trailed off, and her shoulders sagged. "Why would Aunt Jenny mark this with your..."

Willa's chest rose and fell with each deliberate breath. She glanced at Lon's pinched expression and then at the storm raging outside, then back again.

Wait a minute.

Could this book be telling the truth? Actually depicting real-life beings instead of make-believe? Had Aunt Jenny stumbled on something supernatural? Aunt Jenny had always enjoyed reading science fiction and fantasy books, but this was altogether different. This might be real.

Lon gave her a weak smile before cutting his gaze to the window. "While this is fascinating, I need to head out. We can talk about it more later."

Thunder rolled and lightning flashed in the dark ink of night, but the sounds had grown weaker, and the lightning less bright. The storm had finally begun to retreat.

Her fingers tightened on the book, her back straightened, her muscles tensed. Willa sought his gaze. Her bottom lip trembled. The weird tingling from the book's binding intensified. Clarity spread through her mind.

"You!" She bit out. The one word an accusation and demand at the same time. She clambered to her feet and hauled the book with her. She felt like an enraged witch ready to read from her grimoire and curse him to Hell. Lon was a tempest. A water sprite. *Oh my god.* "Was it you?"

"Was what me?"

"The person, the thing, that made Aunt Jenny disappear?"

"Never. Why would I?" His eyes widened before cutting to the window. "And I'm not a thing."

"Well, you're certainly not human," Willa said. "Aunt Jenny discovered the truth and had to be silenced. That's it, isn't it? That's why she's missing. To protect the truth." She lifted the book. "Is that why you're here? To find the book and dispose of the evidence?"

"I can't touch that book. Besides..." Lon took a deep breath. "No one would believe Jenny if she tried to expose us."

She sucked in air. Lon didn't deny what he was, his words practically a confession. He was...he was a water sprite.

Her head grew light, her vision wavered.

"I...I have to go." Lon spun on his heel and ran from the room.

Willa gaped at the doorway Lon had disappeared through. She couldn't believe it. She had trusted this stranger. She'd let him put his hands on her. She'd sucked on his face as if he were the last drop of water in a desert. Even now, she wanted to run after him and call him back. The book said relatively harmless unless protecting their identity.

The pieces fell together. Lon only visited during stormy weather. His face had a pale, otherworldly appearance, and when she'd seen his expression as the lightning streaked outside, she knew. It took less than a minute for her to realize the truth.

Willa clutched the book to her chest and shrieked into the night. Though drowned out by the fading thunder, her cry released some of the chaos inside her head. She felt better, more collected. She closed the book and gently placed it on the shelf, noting the location.

Later, after she'd processed, she'd return to the book and read the tempest section again. Maybe she could find out more about Lon, discover something useful. Plus, the other sticky notes stuck out from the worn pages like little red flags—except they were yellow. Aunt Jenny tagged those pages for a reason, and she wanted to find out why.

She shook her head.

Supernatural creatures? A water sprite? Really?

She must've hit her head harder than she thought. Maybe she'd imagined Lon altogether and she really lay in a coma in some hospital bed somewhere. But that kiss... No, that kiss had touched something deep inside her. Lon was real.

If...if what the book said was true, if Lon and other supernatural beings existed, did it connect to Aunt Jenny's disappearance at all? Despite what she'd learned about Lon, a part of her protested the idea of his involvement with Aunt Jenny going missing.

Willa folded her arms over her chest and plunked down to sit on the floor, in the very spot she would've made love with Lon. The tempest could've easily made her disappear like Aunt Jenny. She'd been alone with him more than once.

If Lon didn't have anything to do with Aunt Jenny going missing, though, who did? Willa glanced at the thick book. Lon's page wasn't the only one marked with a sticky note.

Did her aunt disappear because she'd learned the truth about someone else?

CHAPTER
TEN

"Every joy has a little tease in it, a give and a take,
and leaves a wake of longing."

— SANDY GINGRAS, *HOW TO LIVE
AT THE BEACH*

In her former office-working life, Willa had
Saturday and Sunday off, but with the bookstore
having no other employees, now she only got
Mondays to herself. She used to despise the first day of
the work week—it meant slogging to work only to have
her useless boss order her around.

Once he'd asked her to piece together a receipt he'd
accidentally ripped up so he could claim the fourteen
dollars and twenty-two cents on his monthly expense

form. Another time, he'd called her from his friend's office on the third floor and asked her to fetch a printer cartridge. When she arrived, he'd pointed to the printer and then asked if she knew what to do. She wanted to throttle him, but she also wanted to keep her job. She bit her tongue and like so many other things in her life, she put up with his behavior.

Willa rolled over in bed and stretched, enjoying the release of tension. She always left the window cracked open unless it was exceptionally stormy out and mornings like this were the reason why. The birds sang their sweet songs outside, and a gentle breeze moved through the tree branches, rustling the leaves.

A calm day, brightening under the winter sun, and in complete contrast to the raging storm of emotions flooding her mind. Fear, confusion, disbelief, and yes, lust, flickered through her body as memories from last night resurfaced.

Adopted. She was her father's love child. The certificate hadn't identified the birth parents, but maybe she could get the information from BC records. Mom wouldn't be helpful. She didn't have to ask to know her request for support would be denied. Willa would save that conversation until she had more facts.

Her mind drifted to the weird book. The one with the old parchment paper that tingled her fingers and exposed Lon's true identity as a tempest.

Last night, clutching the book to her chest, everything seemed so clear. Now? Not so much. If she hadn't stumbled over that monstrosity of a book, she would've woken up beside Lon after what would've hopefully been a very satisfying night. If everything had gone well. But it hadn't. She'd downed three cups of tea last night trying to calm her nerves; every tap of a branch, every howl of wind or crash of thunder, made her wonder if an army of water sprites had arrived to kill her fairy-style.

But nobody came. Literally.

With heavy limbs, she'd finally clambered up to bed and flopped face first into the soft pillow. By that point, the fear had dissipated, and she'd accepted what really upset her.

Despite her best efforts, Willa was no closer to finding out what happened to her aunt and her list of suspects had grown almost exponentially. How could she possibly help Aunt Jenny if she didn't even know what was possible?

Did Aunt Jenny discover the truth about Lon on her own or had he told her? If she'd confronted Lon about being a water sprite, it was entirely conceivable that she confronted others.

Maybe Willa was closer to discovering the truth. She had no leads before and now she had a book with a number of marked pages.

She wished...she wished...Gah!

Right now, she wished she hadn't drunk three cups of tea last night. Her early morning routine of staying in bed and enjoying the sheer laziness, was interrupted by the very tangible need to relieve her bladder. She threw the blankets off and sprinted to the bathroom.

When she finally dressed and made her way downstairs, a firm knock on the store's front door made her jump and almost miss a step. With the sun blazing in the blue sky scattered with a few white, fluffy clouds, it couldn't be Lon. Not if she believed what the book said.

Her shoulders sagged and her stomach twisted. She shuffled slowly to the entrance of the store and wished she'd tackled her hair into a bun. At least she'd brushed her teeth.

An RCMP officer studied her as she opened the door. He stood tall at around six feet, with broad shoulders and a narrow waist. His brown hair poked out from under his hat and matching brown eyes softened when she met his gaze. Not just any officer, the same guy who'd witnessed her original missing person's statement and helped her out of the ocean when she'd fallen off that cliff.

Willa's face heated. She didn't know this guy, but he knew an awful lot about her.

"Hello, ma'am. How are you?" Officer Harris' voice held a steely quality. "Have you recovered from your mishap the other day?"

"Y...yes," she replied. Her heart leapt into her throat and stuck there.

"Ms. Eklund, I wanted to stop by to let you know that we're still looking into your aunt's disappearance."

"Oh!" She sagged into the door frame. "I thought you'd come to deliver bad news."

"Sorry to scare you, ma'am. We don't have any leads. Her bank accounts remain untouched, she left her cell phone on these premises, and no one has come forward with any information." Officer Harris' expression softened even more. "We wanted to check in on you to make sure you're doing okay and ask whether anything new has come up since you opened shop."

The stories she could tell...

"I discovered her yellow raincoat and gumboots are missing. I called the office already and gave the information to the person on the phone." Pretty sure Tess shared the "confidential" information already with anyone willing to listen.

The cop's eyebrows rose. He pulled out a notepad and pen from his front pocket and jotted the information down. "I believe I read that report and will follow up on that. Anything else?"

Well, her understanding of the world got dumped upside down and continued to unravel but her personal crisis was hardly relevant to her aunt's case. If supernatural beings were somehow involved, would the police be capable of helping or would they laugh her onto the next ferry off the island? "I'm afraid not."

This officer was a lot nicer than the cranky, older cop she'd dealt with when she first arrived. That man had grilled her for hours about her decision to open the bookstore until she finally confessed her mother didn't want to lose profits from a business she could potentially inherit. The police had left her pretty much alone after that, but the look of judgement on the older man's face still stuck with her.

Willa ran a shaky hand through her hair and started to pull the door closed. "Well, thank you for—"

"Are you okay, ma'am?" Officer Harris leaned in eyes narrowed. "Your head has a pretty good bump."

Willa reached up and pressed the tender skin. "Yeah. I had an argument with a door during the storm a couple nights ago."

"And the door won?"

"I'm afraid so."

Officer Harris pressed his lips together and hesitated. He spoke quietly, barely above a hushed whisper. "Are you sure you're okay? Do you need help? I can get you away from here right away. All you have to do is nod."

Willa's heart picked up the pace, and her palms felt suddenly clammy. Should she tell him about Lon? The book? Would he believe her? An officer of the law stood on her doorstep asking her if she was okay. This was her chance to expose the existence of the supernatural community and their possible involvement with Aunt Jenny's disappearance.

Willa glanced at Officer Harris' chocolate brown eyes and her breathing hitched. No, he'd think she was crazy. Maybe she should find out something more concrete before saying something to the authorities. The sprites may not be involved at all.

"No," she said and tried desperately not to look guilty. Which was ridiculous, because she hadn't done anything wrong.

"Okay." Officer Harris shifted on his feet, back and forth. "You have our number if you change your mind."

She nodded. "Thank you."

He opened his mouth only to shut it again, apparently at a loss of words. "Have you found any journals or notes that might explain your aunt's disappearance?" he asked.

Willa took a moment to catch up to the abrupt change in topic. "No. I wish. I..." She turned away with the sudden sting in her eyes. "I hope she's okay." She turned back to the cop. "I've seen more than one documentary on television about missing persons. They say the first twenty-four hours are crucial. It's been two weeks. I love my aunt and want her home. Is there any hope at all that she's still alive?"

The tension in Officer Harris' shoulders relaxed as he straightened from the doorway. Maybe he heard the truth in her words, too. "There's always hope, ma'am."

CHAPTER
ELEVEN

"The beauty of nature is best known in waves of silence and stillness."

— ANGIE WEILAND-CROSBY

Willa listened to the terrible hold music and held her breath the entire time. She sat at her aunt's small dining table with the long phone cord stretched out to reach.

"Vital Statistics." A woman answered the phone. She sounded tired or perhaps bored. "Margaret speaking."

"Good morning. My name is Willa Eklund and I'm wondering if I can obtain information from my long form birth certificate." She'd practiced what she'd say multiple times before finding the courage to dial the numbers.

"You wish to order a certificate?" Margaret asked.

"I will if I have to."

The woman paused, probably unsure of what she was getting at.

Fair, since Willa wasn't quite sure either.

"I'd like to see the names of the parents listed," she explained.

"Are you adopted? If so, if your birth parent or parents filled out a VSA 632 form, the information will not be available to you, and your adoptive parents could've legally changed the long form birth certificate as well."

She suspected as much when she went through their website, but she had to try something. "I suspect my father had an affair and I'd like to find out who my biological mother is or was."

"Can't you ask him?"

Oh, there were suddenly a lot of questions she wished she could ask Dad. The pain of losing him pierced her heart again. "He passed away ten years ago."

"I'm sorry," Margaret said.

"Thank you." Though the pain was ten years old, it still struck her at times. "I'm just hoping to find some answers. I'll order a certificate, but I'd rather not wait for the mail if that's possible."

"Let's complete an order and I can read the information to you to confirm it's correct." Margaret must be skirting the rules.

"Thank you."

After providing her information, including her credit card number, she waited for Margaret to access her birth certificate information. If this proved to be a dead end, she'd have to let this lead go. Maybe Mom was her biological mother and she'd have to accept her mere existence was offensive to her.

"Okay, let's see here." The woman's keystrokes echoed through their phone connection. "Huh."

Huh? That sounded ominous.

"There's...I'm really sorry, but there's no father listed," Margaret said.

"That can't be right." Willa coiled the phone's long cord around her hand. Or maybe that explained the adoption certificate. Maybe her biological mother hadn't listed Dad and that's why he had to go through the adoption process.

"That's what the certificate says. Your biological mother is listed as Jennifer Skye Eklund and the father isn't listed at all, which means your mom left the field blank on the registration form."

Willa's brain short-circuited. That couldn't be right. She heard the woman wrong. First, she learned supernatural creatures existed and now this woman just old her Aunt Jenny was actually her biological mother.

Oh. My. God. She stood up and paced.

Though shocking, the information fit the clues she found. Why hadn't she seen it sooner? Why hadn't she realized the possibility earlier? Why did Aunt... Why did her biological mother hide this from her and who was her father?

Dad's smiling face popped into her memory. Not her biological father, her uncle. She loved Dad so much. He might not be her biological father, but that changed nothing. Dad had loved her, too. He'd defended her from Mom's sharp tongue and shielded her from her sisters' mean antics. She had a great childhood because of him.

And he'd known the entire time. Why hadn't he told her about Jenny? Why hadn't Mom?

"Ma'am?" Margaret's voice interrupted the stream of questions racing through her head. "Are you okay?"

"Did I hear you right? Jennifer Skye Eklund is listed as my mother?"

"Yes and no second parent is identified. Is this information correct?"

Jenny's face popped up in Willa's memory. Her long wavy hair and bright hazel eyes that always seemed to sparkle with mischief. The sloped nose, arched brows, and high cheekbones they had in common. The willowy frame. Dad always called them two peas in a pod. He said it with love, but now his words had a whole new meaning.

"Yes, I believe so," she told the woman.

"The order is complete. You should receive the certificate in the mail within five business days. Is there anything else I can help you with?"

"No, thank you. You've been very helpful."

Margaret wished her a great day before hanging up. On autopilot, Willa had responded politely and then listened to the dial tone for a few minutes. Maybe ten. Maybe half an hour.

She stood in her aunt's...no...her biological mother's kitchen with the phone cord wrapped around her hand and her body numb.

Jenny was forty-eight years old. That meant she'd been eighteen when she had Willa. Had she given Willa up because she felt she was too young for the responsibility? But why hadn't she said anything? Especially after Dad died.

Speaking of which, why did Mom and her evil daughters keep quiet? They had to know, too. The whole family told the story about how Mom was pregnant with Willa during Dad's sabbatical. They'd been living overseas when Mom had gone into labour. They all told the story. The fabricated lie. Why? They had ample opportunity to push her farther from their lives all this time and remained silent instead.

Willa untangled her hand from the cord and hung up the phone.

Mind still reeling, she walked to the counter to fill a bottle of water. If her family knew her true parentage, did that also mean they were aware of her biological father's identity? Or was there a more sinister reason for him not to be listed on her birth certificate?

Willa set the kettle aside. She didn't want to sit and think. Too much turmoil broiled inside her. The ocean might not hold any more answers than it did the day before or the day before that, but she'd stare at it anyway and find the familiar comfort from each wave.

CHAPTER
TWELVE

"A vacation to the ocean swims you deep into the past; when summer spun her beauty into moments meant to last."

— ANGIE WEILAND-CROSBY

30 YEARS AGO...

Skye swiped at the tears running down her face and tried not to look at the shack they'd pulled up to. She'd signed the adoption forms over an hour ago, yet she still hadn't fully recovered.

"Are you sure about this?" her brother asked from the driver's seat. "We can just work with the current system."

She tried to laugh, but it came out as a choked sob. "There's no way your wife would ever help raise a child that's not hers, especially if she knew Willa was mine. We need this so Willa will be loved by her whole family."

"She's not that bad."

"She hates me."

Tony winced. Fifteen years her senior, he'd always walked a fine line between acting as her older brother and a third parent.

"And..." She took a deep breath. "And I don't want to remember. I'll hate myself for my weakness and... and the grief will be unbearable."

Tony sucked in a deep breath.

"But I'll be the best aunt." She bobbed her head, almost believing it. "I know I will."

"Skye..."

She shook her head. "Just promise me you'll love her."

"I already do. Like my own."

"And promise me you'll keep her away from the ocean as much as you can."

"I've already promised, but I promise again. She'll have a happy, ordinary life." He turned the ignition off. "But this? Isn't this a little extreme?"

She bit her lip. She didn't know if her lover would ever come looking for her. She didn't know what the ramifications were for having his child. She needed to protect her baby, hiding her among humans, and at the same time, trying to find some way to mend her own broken heart. This was the best solution she could think of.

"What will this cost you?" Concern crinkled her brother's brow.

"Her fees are quite reasonable."

Tony narrowed his eyes at her. "You know what I mean."

"The cost of the fairy spell to have your family accept Willa as their own is my memory of her and her father." She gulped. "Rather fitting. I was going to ask for that anyway. I think I'm getting the better deal."

Tony pursed his lips.

"And almost half my savings, but it's worth it." She reached out and placed her hand on his arm. All he ever did was try to protect her.

"I need to do this," she said. "The pain...The pain is too much. It's like a part of me left when he did, and it hasn't returned. Not even Willa has made me feel whole again. I look at her and feel guilty, guilty for hoping she'll fix me, guilty for hoping she'll somehow bring him back, and guilty for...for hating her a little for doing neither of those things." She twisted her shirt in her hands. She couldn't mention the fear of what would happen if the true identity of her father was discovered. "I'm the worst mother."

"No, you're not. A lot of mothers feel down after giving birth. Maybe you should talk to—"

"Stop." She held up her hand. "I know you mean well, but I would feel better knowing she's loved and safe with you. This is the best solution to a troubling situation, the option that still allows me to know and love her. Despite all my other feelings, I love her. I love her so much. I want what's best for her."

His expression softened.

"And I know that means giving her up."

"But not entirely." He flashed her a small smile. "You've already proven you're the best aunt to my other children."

She drew in a shaky breath and nodded. "Let's go talk to the sea witch."

CHAPTER
THIRTEEN

"Hope greeted me on the horizon with a warm gleaming smile."

— ANGIE WEILAND-CROSBY

CURRENT DAY...

Willa sat on a rock formation jutting out from the shore. The wind whipped her hair and the smell of sea foam and seaweed curled around her with the cold. The ocean beckoned her to come forward, tugging at something deep inside. Like always, she ignored it. Her father had raised her to be wary of the dangerous waters, opting for swimming pools and lakes during the summer instead of the ocean.

Her phone vibrated in her pocket, and she sighed.

Only one person called her these days and the conversations never left her with warm fuzzy feelings. Today's chat would be no different.

She pulled the phone from her pocket and accepted the call. "Hello, *Mother*."

"Today is your day off and yet I haven't received a report," she said as a greeting.

"Did you know?" Willa asked. Of course, Mom knew. Babies didn't spontaneously appear without explanation.

"Know what?" Mom snapped.

"That Dad adopted me and you're not my biological mother?"

A long, drawn-out pause answered her. Mom didn't run out of words often, but when she did, the silence scared Willa.

"How dare you," she finally hissed.

"What?"

"How dare you say such a thing. How could a child of mine be so ungrateful? I raised you better."

Willa frowned and stared at her phone screen. Had a demon somehow possessed it during the call?

"Did you finally figure out what a payload the bookstore is?" Mom continued. "Is that it? Is that why you've delayed sending the reports? You're hoping you're named in Jenny's will and plan to cut us out."

Willa dropped her mouth open. What the hell was Mom talking about?

"You better watch yourself, young lady, or I'll make

sure you get nothing from Jenny's estate when it inevitably passes to us. I doubt that flake of an aunt even has a will."

"She's not my aunt."

"That's enough. I don't know what game you're playing, but—"

"She's my biological mother."

Mom sucked in a breath and what followed was another pause scarier than the last.

"I'm not saying this because of some scheme to get an inheritance," Willa said. "I found an adoption certificate and my long form birth certificate lists Jenny as my mother, not you."

Mom remained silent.

"You had to have known, right? Do you know who my biological father is or why he wasn't listed on the certificate? Dad's gone now. Surely you can tell me the truth."

"The only thing I'm sure of is you've been partaking in some of those recreational drugs the island is so well known for. No amount of wishful thinking will alter your birth. Trust me. I'd know." Mom hung up before Willa could say anything else, but really, what more was there to say? Mom didn't know. How was that possible? How had Dad tricked her?

Willa shoved the phone in her pocket. She rested her elbows on her knees and held her head up with her hands. The wind continued to play with her hair and the rising tide teased the tips of her boots. She'd have to leave this spot soon or the ocean would cover her path back and she'd have to swim.

The wind whistled past her, and the seagulls called in the distance. The rippling ocean whispered to her. *Dive in.*

She shook her head and stood. She needed to get back to the store and hopefully, find a reality that made sense along the way.

FOURTEEN

"On the shore of nature's magic, I dreamed summer knew no end."

— ANGIE WEILAND-CROSBY

F ive weeks since Aunt Jenny's disappearance, and still no word. With each day that passed delivering clear skies and calm seas, Willa's mood plummeted. It had been two weeks since the last storm rocked Gabriola Island.

She wanted to see Lon. Surely, he would've told her if he knew her true parentage, however, he had other answers. Ones that had nothing to do with Jenny and everything to do with who and what he was. Would he visit her again? Or would he avoid her because of how things ended the last time they saw each other?

With today's forecast calling for cloud cover and a looming threat of thunderstorms, she'd hopefully get her wish.

With the bookstore closed, she spent the day wandering around town and thinking about what she'd say to Lon.

After stopping by the coffee shop, Willa drifted around Gabriola's one and only mall—a horseshoe shaped string of stores nestled within the loop of the main road that circled the island.

"Hello, dear!" An older woman with flaming red hair in an up-knot sat on one of the benches in the area outside the art gallery and waved her arm in the air. Ms. Murphy.

Willa smiled and waved back.

"C'mere, lass! Tell me, have you seen Alice?"

"No." She straightened to look around. "Did you want me to find her?"

"Gosh no." The older woman waved in the air. "How are ye?"

"Good." Willa gripped her coffee cup and walked over to join the Scottish woman on the bench. The potent aroma of the nearby restaurant flooded her senses and made her mouth water. The establishment served a variety of food from fish and chips and burgers to pizza and pasta.

"How are you, Ms. Murphy? Feeling better?"

"Aye! Just dandy," she said, and then held up a familiar book. "I hear you're to thank for this book. Brilliant piece."

"You're welcome. Hey, I've been meaning to ask you. I met someone on the island named Lon and Alice mentioned you might know him."

"Lon? No. But I love that name. Means fierce and when I was a young lass, I loved a boy named Lon." The older woman's gaze drifted off.

"What happened?"

"Huh?" Ms. Murphy visibly shook herself. "Oh, well. Not much. We were just kids, and he didn't know I existed."

"I'm sorry."

"Psssst child." Ms. Murphy waved her hand away as if to ward off Willa's words.

"Well, I'm glad you like the book."

"Oh, I do. Listen to this." The short and rotund woman began to regale her with the explicit sections of the book in her heavy Scottish brogue.

Willa squirmed in her seat as Ms. Murphy read about heaving bosoms, swollen members, and quivering mounds. It took three fairly graphic scenes and a promise to visit before Willa extracted herself from the verbal clutches of the older woman.

"Lass!" Ms. Murphy called out to her before she could fully escape.

Willa cringed and turned around to find the other

woman leaning forward and squinting, her lurid book momentarily forgotten.

"Yes?" Willa asked.

"You have the look of the fae in you girl."

"Oh." Willa straightened and scratched her head. "Thanks?"

"Ye need to be careful in these parts, lass. The fairy folk are fickle." The woman shook her head, eyes glazing into a foggy look before she picked up her book and continued to read, as if Willa no longer existed or the exchange never happened.

"Fairy folk?" Willa asked. "On Gabriola Island?"

Ms. Murphy shook her head, as if momentarily confused by Willa's comment. Or disappointed in it. "The fae are everywhere lass. In the woods, the seas and even in the skies. Just stay away from that old witch. She's taken an interest in ye."

"Witch?" She scoffed. "Surely there's no such thing." Though why was she surprised? If tempests existed, if someone could brainwash her identity from her entire family and have them believe she belonged to them, surely an evil witch wasn't that outlandish.

"Oh, she's a real witch, all right. A sea witch. Cruel and calculating and hiding behind a fake veneer. She'll sell you seashells and have you believe they're gold."

Okay then.

"Thank you for the warning," Willa said despite the questions rebounding in her mind. Who was the witch? Where was the witch located? What did the witch do? So many questions, yet a part of her still didn't quite accept the existence of the supernatural. Part of her wanted to believe Ms. Murphy had one too many screws loose. And another part of her hoped if she kept her head in the sand just a little bit longer, her world would return to normal.

The old woman nodded and pulled something from her pocket. With a deep breath, she held a smooth gray stone out in her open palm. "For you."

Willa looked down at the rock with a naturally made hole in the centre. "I've seen one of these before."

"Have ye now?"

She nodded. "In Jenny's cash register."

Ms. Murphy froze. Everything around them stilled as if frozen in time along with the older woman's breathing. "Did you move it?"

"Not really. It was causing the drawer to jam so I relocated it to another place inside the register. Why? Did I do something wrong?"

Ms. Murphy sighed, and her posture lost its stiffness. The world around them came alive again. "I gave that to your aunt to protect her from the sea witch."

Poor woman. She was obviously delusional.

Ms. Murphy jutted her hand out once again. "Take it."

"What exactly is it?" With everything else in her life, she hadn't had a chance to search on the internet for more information.

"A hag stone."

Willa frowned. Certainly, the woman wasn't implying either of them was a hag.

"It's for protection," Ms. Murphy explained.

Well, how could she argue against that? She smiled and plucked the stone from the older woman's hand and slid it into her pocket. "Thank you."

"Keep it with you, dear."

Willa raised her now-empty coffee cup in a silent salute and hustled away before Ms. Murphy started serenading her with her favorite book sections again or lurid tales of the fae.

With the light fading fast, Willa decided to visit the Malaspina Galleries. She parked and chucked her wallet into the centre console. The last thing she wanted was to accidentally drop something into the water. Crime was practically non-existent on Gabe, especially during the off-season. Her lack of coordination was more certain than theft, so she prepared accordingly.

She got out of the vehicle, shut the door, and locked it before heading for the short trail to the cliffs.

The sky grew dark with ominous clouds, but not enough for a storm, not yet. The changing weather left her apprehensive, nervous and excited all at the same time. She needed to know if the sprites were involved with her aunt's disappearance. She needed Lon.

She didn't know what she'd say to him, but at least she didn't have to worry about that tonight. She'd done some research on the internet. According to a number of sites, tempests needed thunder and lightning to take human form. The weather forecast called for light drizzle, if anything, and that wouldn't be enough for Lon to appear.

Malaspina Galleries was a sandstone cave formed by the ocean along one side of a bay. The whole length of the cave opened up allowing visitors to walk through it and feel as though they travelled under a frozen wave.

Seagulls cried out, possessive and nerve-grating as ever. She climbed down the rocks to get closer to cool ocean water. The tide was up and gently lapping the lower level of the cave. Her boots splashed in the puddles forming along the sandstone surface.

Willa rolled her shoulders and gazed at the deep blue sea as it almost merged with the darkening sky. She'd always loved the way the ocean breeze combed through her hair, even on a mild day.

Maybe her love for the ocean was why she felt such a strong connection to Lon. "It doesn't make sense," she said, speaking quietly to her feet. "How can I feel this way?"

Did the water swirl more at her feet? No, purely her imagination. She'd imagined a lot of things in these last few weeks.

"I read the rest of the book," she told the sea. "Apparently, tempests are pretty badass when they're pissed, but I'm angry, too, you know. Maybe I misread you and that kiss, but why didn't you tell me?

Why did you run? If you didn't take Aunt Jenny, who did?"

Again, the ocean held no answers, but the wind picked up. The ocean swelled against the opening of the cave before crashing hard against the shoreline farther down.

The breeze ruffled through her hair, and she splashed the cold water with her boots.

"If tempests exist, could other, nastier creatures roam around? The book certainly thinks so, and if it was right about you..." If someone else found out about Jenny's knowledge, or discovered she had that book maybe they would do something to her to ensure her silence.

The chill of the incoming storm spiralled around her. She shuddered. If that were true, Aunt Jenny might be gone forever. Dead.

And all her answers with her.

Willa crouched down to trail her fingers in the surging ice-cold water. Her eyes stung and for once, she didn't stop the tears from falling. The droplets hit the water below her and created little ripples on the dark blue surface.

A reflection of her face stared back at her, broken by the increased swell of the water. The waves, almost non-existent when she first arrived, grew in intensity. If only they would bring a storm.

She might never see Lon again, and the thought sent searing pain to her heart.

"I know you're not here to answer, but I wonder, Lon. Did you put some sort of spell on me? Enthrall me with some crazy supernatural voodoo? How can I feel the way I do when I've only met you a few times?" With the deep blue withholding its knowledge, Willa picked herself up to walk back to the car. Her day off almost over, and she felt more lost than ever.

"Wait!" A whisper floated in the breeze.

Willa spun around and peered into the water, now a deep, blue-black with only the moon to light its depths. The choppy water distorted the surface, but a translucent object solidified from the depths of the ocean. Lon's pale face appeared in the water below.

Willa gasped.

With his chin tilted up toward her, submerged in the water, Lon's storm-gray eyes met hers. She shook her head and looked again. His lips moved under the water, as if he spoke to her. She leaned closer.

"Not...spell... Not a spell..."

Willa's hand flew to her mouth, and she quickly inhaled. She reached down to pull him out of the water, but his face disappeared, melting into the deep blue as if he'd never existed. Overextended, she toppled forward.

"Ahh!" Willa flapped her arms and tried to correct her balance, but it was too late. Her body hit the ocean with an icy slap. Her forehead struck a rock. Pain lanced across her face.

The water swirled around her, angry and dark.

Her arms flailed as she tried to find a rhythm with her legs to stay afloat. She lacked control. The cold chopped at her face, and she gulped down seawater. No! This wasn't supposed to happen.

The water continued to crash against her, slamming her body into the rocks. Her head smacked a jagged edge and her vision, already poor in the fading light, narrowed, until only darkness and one thought remained.

Lon?

Her body began to float upward. She opened her mouth to take a breath and quickly shut it. Her throat contracted and awareness flittered back. Her body had contorted into an awkward position with her torso arched forward and her limbs back, like the air trapped in her lungs fought to get out.

She moved her arms. Despite her fascination with the ocean, she'd never been a strong swimmer.

Do something.

She opened her mouth again letting out a little bit of air while she kicked and thrashed. She needed to conserve oxygen. The cold water sucked the energy from her limbs and made them unresponsive.

Everything was dark. Was she heading in the right direction? Which way was up?

She stopped foundering, stopped moving.

Pressure built in her lungs, painful and stabbing. She drifted in the current and began to float upward again.

Okay. This way is up.

She started kicking her legs. They didn't respond like they should. The pain in her chest became unbearable. The need to inhale burned from within.

And then suddenly, it was all gone. The pain, the burn, the urge to escape the ocean.

Her body went limp and her mind blank. She gave up, letting the numbness spread through her body. Cool tingling spread until a sense of warmth replaced it. Willa drifted in the ocean current and opened her mouth, drawing water in.

Agony erupted within her.

Her back arched as searing pain ripped open her skin. Clothes shredded as her body reformed. Her pants fell away and drifted to the ocean floor. A burning sensation raced through her body as if she'd caught on fire. Her legs snapped shut as if polarized magnets pulled them together. Scales pushed through the skin on her legs and her feet elongated into one large tail fin. It glistened with an incandescent shine. Her lower half had transformed completely, covered with scales that ended just below her belly button. She shouldn't be seeing any of this. Either her eyesight had improved to provide underwater vision or her scales glowed brightly enough to illuminate everything.

She moved her legs. No. Wait. That wasn't right. Her tail. She moved her tail. It swished through the water in response, and she squealed. Bubbles escaped her mouth.

She shut it again.

Wait a minute. How was she breathing? She floated in the mid-ocean column. Muscles contracted and relaxed near her lower back. She patted her body, feeling her cold skin until she got to the curve of her lower spine. Just above where the scales of her tail ended, deep slits lined her back, running at the same angle as her ribs.

Gills.

She had gills.

And a tail.

She twisted around in the water, her hair flowing around her.

I'm a mermaid.

CHAPTER
FIFTEEN

"In the ocean, I slip from my skin into the soul of the sea."

— ANGIE WEILAND-CROSBY

Willa's shredded shirt caught in her gills, bunching up in the slits and sending pain streaking up and down her back. She gasped for air. Tearing the fabric from her body, she let it float away in the underwater current.

Her bra kept her breasts from bobbing in the water, but the clasp rubbed the top end of her first gill slits, so she popped off the undergarment and surrendered it to the ocean as well. Maybe this explained how tempests found clothing to wear for their trips to land.

How did this even happen? How was this possible?

Slowly, she turned in the ocean and took in her surroundings.

The seabed glowed orange and white from a massive number of plumose anemones. Ranging in size from a couple of inches to a few feet, the anemones transformed the ocean floor and sandstone rocks into a colourful display.

Long kelp leaves swayed in the underwater current as if dancing to a silent tune. She swayed along with them, her scalp tingling as her hair joined the dance.

A large red crab scurried across the ocean floor. She dove toward it, but lost sight of the crustacean in the kelp forest. She scanned the area but found no more crabs to follow.

A grey head poked out from a break in the anemones and sunflower sea stars coating the sandstone rock face. She swished backward in surprise. With a face only a mother could love, a giant wolf eel slowly emerged from its rocky burrow. The head of its mate poked out and followed. The two eels swam around her, their smooth bodies sliding past. She swayed with them, stretching out her arms. The male swam below her outstretched arm and butted her palm with his head. She smiled and ran her hand down his body. The moment ended and the eels returned to their burrow. She'd never imagined experiencing something so beautiful in her life.

A few lingcod swam past her, and she turned to watch them disappear into the forest. Something else caught her eye. A shape floated between her and the disappearing fish. Not really a shape, so much as an awareness, a presence, faintly outlined with a bioluminescent glow.

She'd know that shape anywhere.

Lon? Her arms instinctively twitched to cover her chest. She folded them over her boobs.

This is a lovely surprise. Lon's deep voice spoke in her head.

You can hear me?

Of course. I can hear all of Triton's descendants.

Who?

He cocked is head. *Did you not know? I wondered when I saw you thrashing around.*

You saw me drown? Why didn't you save me?

He bowed his head. *I've always sensed you were something more than human, but I didn't know your exact lineage. I don't have the ability to help humans in this form.*

But I'm not human. She spoke the thought as soon as it entered her brain and then the implications hit her. She wasn't human.

Lon swayed in the ocean flows and didn't answer right away. He floated toward her and reached out. His hand pressed against her cheek as if made of flesh and bone. Her skin heated from the contact and the now-familiar tingling danced along her face. Maybe they had more than chemistry. Maybe the interaction of their supernatural natures caused the tingling sensation. Maybe Willa was a complete idiot.

Not fully human, he answered. *Not fully Tritian, either.*

I'm Jenny's daughter.

He paused as though momentarily at a loss for words. They bobbed in the ocean as he visibly processed the information. Finally, he spoke. *That explains your mother's hostility.*

That was not what she expected him to say. *How exactly does that explain my mother's attitude toward me?*

He spoke slowly at first, as if carefully selecting his words. *Placing a supernatural child into a human home has never gone well, historically,* he said. *The fae call them changelings. Despite powerful magic, the foster mother always instinctively knows when the child is not her own. That usually manifests in anger and hatred toward the child no matter how lovely or well-behaved.*

Willa's stomach twisted in another knot. Mom's animosity was unforgiveable, but maybe that explanation could help Willa heal the emotional wounds the woman had inflicted over the years. *You think Jenny placed the spell over me? To hide me within the family?*

Jenny wouldn't have laid the spell. He stopped short. *Jenny's human. Fully human.*

Are you sure?

He nodded. *She has a human aura, which means your father must hail from Triton's line. You have always had the most alluring aura.*

How did she respond to that? Was that why his skin always seemed to zap her? Because of her aura?

Wait a minute. Did you say Triton? She'd heard the name of course. She might be a hermit by nature, but she read books, she watched movies. *Do you mean King Triton?*

He's the king of the sea and the son of Poseidon.

She bobbed in the ocean, drawing cool ocean water through her gills. What did that make her? The possible answers scared her, and she wasn't ready to hear what Lon would say about it. Her arms tightened around her chest.

Where do you get your clothes? she blurted out. Apparently, she needed a lesson on prioritizing.

I have clothes stashed on various beaches in this area. Some, I've had to steal. Some were lost to the ocean when I found them. Others are gifted to me by the few select humans, like Jenny, who know of my existence. Or I borrow from my brothers.

Brothers?

I told you I had a few. We generally live solitary lives, but we often get together during storms to enjoy the upwelling of magic...kind of like a party, but the drinks are made of power instead of alcohol.

No sisters?

Lon frowned. She sensed his effort to find the right words more than she saw a change in expression. *All tempests are male.*

Why? How do you reproduce then?

His form solidified even more, enough to make out the twist of his lips. *Why are you so interested in our reproduction?*

I'm trying to make sense of it. How do you survive as a species?

Tempests are not born, we are made. We were created by Poseidon. He used his power to form us in his image from the elemental magic of the ocean. That's why all tempests are male. Lon drifted closer, his hands running up her arms. *Unlike my kind, you're ocean royalty. All merpeople are.*

What I am is confused. And overwhelmed. The joy of meeting the eels and seeing Lon slipped away, replaced with icy dread. Royalty? Her? *I want to go home.*

It's a lot to take in. Lon nodded and held his hand out. *Let's get you home. I'll take you back to the galleries, but you'll have to travel the rest of the way on your own.*

She stared at his open palm. *How?*

On your feet.

She swung her tail around and stared at it pointedly.

If you're anything like Triton's children, you'll gain

your human form once you draw air back into your lungs.

She slowly unfolded one of her arms, still covering her chest with the other, and reached out to take Lon's offered hand. *Does that mean I have to drown every time I want to be a mermaid?*

Something like that. But now you know death will not greet you, but an underwater world, instead. Maybe that will make it more bearable.

The memory of the pain and pressure resurfaced, and she shivered. *Doubtful.*

Lon squeezed her hand and led her to a wall of sandstone covered with seaweed and sea anemones.

The other night, you asked me what I wanted, she said.

His outline wavered as if emotion shook through him. *I remember.*

What do you want? Why are you helping me?

I want you to be happy.

That's not quite what I asked.

I want... His outline shook again. *I want companionship, love, and a sense of belonging. I've been searching for this my entire existence, and for the first time, I'm hopeful that it's actually a possibility.*

Woah. *With a burnt-out, rejected book nerd?*

You are so much more than that. He sighed and pointed up. *Your home awaits.*

CHAPTER
SIXTEEN

"Summer strummed on a lonely shore, "My heart is young; but my soul feels worn."

— ANGIE WEILAND-CROSBY

What the hell just happened? Willa clambered up the rocky shore, naked and shaking. The fresh air had burned her lungs just as Lon suspected. Her tail had ripped apart and her legs reformed. She slipped on the wet rocks and crashed onto the uneven ground. Her ears rang and more pain lanced through her lungs. She took a deep breath and pushed up. This time, her bare feet found purchase and she pulled herself upright.

A giant wave splashed against the rocky ledge beside her. When the water retreated, it revealed her car keys and hag stone. Lon must've retrieved them from the ocean floor. Unlike her ripped clothes, the keys and stone would've sunk almost straight down instead of getting carried away by the current.

She plucked the items from the ground and turned back to the ocean, covering her chest again by folding her arms over her exposed breasts. If Lon waited in the waves, she couldn't detect his presence. "Thank you."

The stone mocked her where it lay in her palm. Willa snorted. Some protection charm. This thing had let her drown.

Sort of.

She shivered and ran her free hand up and down her arm. The events that led to this moment still spiraled through her mind. Too outrageous. Too preposterous. Yet, she couldn't deny that she now stood soaking wet and naked along the rocky shore, unscathed from near drowning.

Before her brain combusted, she stumbled to the deserted parking lot on wobbly legs. With a belly full of ocean water and a heart full of lead, she opened the car door and slipped inside.

She'd grown a tail.

Gills.

Holy fuck, she was a mermaid.

How could she not know she was a mermaid? Why

didn't Jenny tell her? Or Dad? Lon said Jenny's aura was human, which only created more questions. Did Jenny and Dad know Willa's biological father was from the sea? Did this have anything to do with Jenny's disappearance or Willa's adoption?

Willa took deep breaths and tried to slow her rapidly beating heart and racing mind. Luckily, her car predated battery-operated key fobs, otherwise, she'd be stranded in the parking lot...naked. Guess owning an older vehicle had its perks. With a shaky hand, she inserted the key into the ignition and turned it. The engine roared to life.

Maybe she had imagined it all. Maybe she had become concussed from all the head trauma and somehow, with the aid of extraordinary hallucinations, managed to save herself from drowning?

No.

She drowned.

The memory of the ache and pain from the water filling her lungs flared up. She drowned and then sprouted a tail and gills. Lon had found her and helped her return to shore. Lon—

Lon, a water sprite who dissolved in water like sugar and wanted companionship and love. With her.

Nothing about this situation was normal.

Her throat tightened. It had to be a dream. Had to be. And she'd been fool enough to fall for it. Literally.

The pain in her head subsided a little and sank

down to her chest. With no blanket in the car, she'd have to drive home naked. Fantastic. The only thing preventing her from sitting in the car, immobile with embarrassment was the innate knowledge the more she delayed, the more likely she'd have witnesses.

Willa shook off some of the water and shifted the gear out of park. Her head throbbed, and she reached up to tenderly touch the right side of her skull as she drove toward home. Her hands came away bloody. Just great. There'd be a goose egg the size of a golf ball on the side of her head by tomorrow morning. A nice little reminder of her foolishness.

Like she needed another one.

When she reached the store, she almost slammed on the brakes. A man rested his shoulder against the door with his back to her. At a stocky five foot eight, with clean cut, light brown hair, the man wore beige slacks, a green polo shirt and loafers, like a preppy college kid despite being in his mid-thirties. George.

Ice flowed through her veins, as if the cold water dripping from her naked and numb body somehow reached inside her. She took a deep breath, parked the car and got out.

George turned at her approach and his teeth flashed. "Why are you naked?"

"A misadventure at the beach." Every cell in her body screamed at her to cover up, but the nearest clothing was inside.

"It's certainly a way to greet perspective

customers." His smooth voice grated her nerves. Condescending and arrogant, as always. He leaned in and without hesitation, or permission, planted a warm kiss on her cheek. "Hello, darling."

"What do you want?" Her shoulders drooped and the weariness of her near-drowning set in. She was so tired. Her feet grew heavy as cement blocks and anchored her in place. All she wanted to do was climb up to her room and sleep for a million years. She crossed her arms over her exposed chest.

George's smile faltered. Then his gaze travelled her body from head to foot and back again. "Have you joined a nudist colony? I hear there's one on the island."

"Honestly, George? You came all the way from Van to scold me on my appearance?" She shouldered past him and unlocked the door. Yeah, she was naked as the day she was born, but George had no business judging her. She wanted to go inside, get warm, get dressed and curl up with a hot chocolate.

Maybe even cry a little and feel sorry for herself.

"No, I..." George ran a hand through his short hair and glanced around. "Can we talk inside?"

That was the last thing she wanted. Playing host to a certifiable d-bag ranked pretty low on her list of priorities right now. He'd come all this way, though, and curiosity gnawed at her gut. Maybe he'd finally explain himself. Her breath caught. Maybe even apologize.

"Sure," she said. "You can wait downstairs in the

kitchen while I take a hot shower and find some clothes."

George's shoulders straightened, and he flashed her another quick smile, this one a little more genuine than the last.

Whatever.

She left him downstairs with the task of making hot drinks before she escaped to her sanctuary.

WILLA DIDN'T WAIT for the water to get hot before jumping into the shower. Anything was warmer than her current state. Soon enough, the heat hit her skin and she sighed in relief. The hot shower soothed her nerves, and if she cried a little from confusion, anger and a weird sense of loss, no one would be the wiser.

After thick steam filled the entire bathroom and the last prickles of cold had left her body, she turned off the shower and started dressing. Alone in her bedroom, she chose George's least favorite clothes—the teal green shirt he said made her look pregnant, and the dark denim skinny jeans he claimed made her look stubby. Before she left the room, she glanced in the mirror and gave herself a thumbs up.

"About time." George looked up when she reached the bottom of the stairs. He sat on the same kitchenette chair Lon had taken, looking smaller and weak in comparison. Leaning back, he'd sprawled his legs out in front of him. With one arm draped over the back of the chair, the other rested on the table, he drummed his fingers on the dark oak. His eyebrows pinched together giving him a pensive look, one she was well acquainted with. The wind picked up outside and the sounds of heavy rain and the occasional foghorn filled the night.

"Excuse me?" she asked.

"What took you so long?"

Willa took a deep breath and headed for the kettle to flick it on. She peered at the clock. She'd taken an hour but gave zero fucks that George had to wait for her. "I'm no longer on your schedule, George. Say what you came to say."

"No longer..." George straightened on the chair. He looked down at his now folded hands.

Willa snorted and went to get a mug. He hadn't made anything. How typical. He rarely ever did something for her, even if she asked multiple times. His gifts always came with strings. He didn't give without the expectation of receiving, he always wanted something in return. Or, as she found out later, he also gave gifts when the small amount of conscience he had left felt bad about his behaviour.

"I want you back," he said.

Willa's hand froze halfway to the cupboard. She let it drop to her side and slowly turned around. George's hazel eyes met hers, deep and sincere. Had he crawled back to her three weeks ago, before she met Lon, she probably would've run to him. But now? She studied his face, one she used to find handsome, and felt...nothing.

George's mouth flattened. "Aren't you going to say something?"

"You want me back?" Willa said.

"That's what I said."

"No apology?"

"Apology?" he asked, his tone incredulous, like he couldn't fathom what he had to be sorry for.

"For leaving me broken-hearted while you ran off with my best friend. How's Colleen, anyway?"

He flinched. "Colleen and I are done. We had irreconcilable differences."

"You discovered she had an opinion?" Surprising.

George leaned forward.

Willa braced for his outrage. He hated her talking back. Always said if he wanted her opinion, he'd ask for it. What had she ever seen in this man? She never should've wasted so many years on him.

Then something weird happened. His body relaxed into the old chair, and the almost-sincere smile spread across his face.

"She wasn't you," he said.

"You left me," she pointed out.

"Well, that wasn't all on me. Part of my leaving was really your own—"

"My own what? Fault?" She raised one eyebrow.

"Willa, I love you. I want you back, but you need to be more understanding of my needs. I thought maybe we could work on that, you know, together. Start fresh."

"Your needs?" she said, more to herself than to George. "All I did was look after and care for your needs. Never mind."

George sat back in his chair. "And I love that about you, I do. But you also need to have your own things, give me space to breathe."

Willa squeezed her eyes shut and counted to ten. When that didn't work, she kept going to one hundred.

"Willa?"

One hundred and thirty-four...

"Willa!"

One hundred and fifty-two...

"Willa! Will you look at me?"

She opened her eyes and studied George's open expression. Some of her anger dissipated. He may not have uttered the word, "sorry," but she knew how much it had cost him to come down here and ask her to come back. He cared for her, she knew that, but was it enough?

"Will you answer me?" George asked.

"No," she said.

George nodded his head. "Fine, you need time. I get that. I'll stay in one of the—"

"I meant no I won't come back. There will be no starting over. No us."

George's eyebrows disappeared into his hairline and his eyes widened. "No?"

"No." She deserved so much more than what he had to offer. She didn't need a man for money, she had a job. Sort of. If she needed companionship, she could get a dog. And sexually? She'd never relied on George to get her off before, why start now?

George took another deep breath and stood from the table. "Willa, you're obviously not in the right state of mind. You've had a rough day. I can't go anywhere tonight, anyway. I missed the last ferry. I'll take one of the spare rooms, stay a couple of days, and maybe you'll change your mind. Will you have dinner with me tomorrow? Maybe you could tell me what happened tonight to leave you looking like a naked shipwreck?"

The tension left Willa's shoulders. His dinner invitation and reasonable request surprised her. Maybe he had changed. But it didn't matter. She had changed as well. Mentally and physically.

"No," she repeated. "You can go find a room somewhere else or you can sleep in your car, but you're not staying here." He didn't deserve her empathy, time or space, and she didn't owe him a goddamn thing.

"Everything will be closed. I waited for you for hours," he growled.

"Plenty of time to sort out accommodations."

He pushed in the chair, jostling the table. His gaze flashed with anger and something else. He took a deep breath and released his tight grip on the back of the chair. "Fine. I'll go for now, but I'd like to see you tomorrow."

"I'll check my schedule."

He snarled and stalked out of the bookstore, slamming the door behind him.

CHAPTER
SEVENTEEN

"Summer kisses the salty sea with hope, and
sunlight, and waves of glee."

— ANGIE WEILAND-CROSBY

Willa slipped from Bound to Please in the
early morning hours. She locked the
door. Thankfully, George hadn't
camped out on the front step. If she
could avoid him for the rest of the day, she'd count
herself lucky.

Normally, she opened the shop in a couple of
hours, but she placed a sign on the door letting
prospective customers know she'd be closed for the
day. Willa needed time to think. Her dreams last night

were filled with fish, kelp, starfish, and Lon. She needed to prove whether the whole thing was a hallucination from head trauma or if she truly was a daughter of the sea.

She walked down Berry Point Road until she reached a rectangular slab of cement with the top spray-painted yellow to mark the public access trail. This path led to Pilot Bay. She followed the gentle winding trail through the forest of fir and arbutus trees. The underbrush of salal and giant ferns lined the needle ridden path until it opened up five hundred meters to the sandstone beach.

The tide was in and gently lapping at the rock formations at the base of the trail. While staying within the protection of the giant trees, Willa pulled her clothes off and tucked them under a giant fern leaf. The wind gently flowed over her exposed skin, and she shivered standing there in her bathing suit.

She chose this location mainly because of its proximity to home, her familiarity with the beach and its relative privacy. Though houses speckled both sides of the heavily forested bay, she hoped no one was paying too much attention to this spot as the sun began to rise. Most people were still asleep or at least in that early morning fog trying to get ready for the day.

Even if someone did spot her, they'd assume she was just another free spirit who liked to suffer early morning dips in frigid water.

Willa took a deep breath, scrambled down the rocks and slipped into the ice-cold water.

Oooo, that's cold.

She sucked in a breath and pulled her bathing suit off under the water. Balling the material in one hand, she threw it onto the shore. It hit a dry sandstone mound with a wet slap. Before she could question her sanity, she dove beneath the surface and grabbed one of the formations jutting from the bottom of the sandstone bank.

Time to either drown or discover her alter ego truly existed.

Holding onto the rock, she squeezed her eyes shut and opened her mouth, exhaling all her air and then drawing in the salty water.

Pain shot through her back and down her legs. Her body pulsed as her legs fused together and gills split open her back. The throb and sting of the transformation wasn't as bad as last time.

Lon had been right.

She hadn't imagined any of it.

Her tail formed and she studied it under the brightening light. Green, blue, and purple, the scales shone and changed colour with the weak bands of the early morning winter sun.

Willa smiled and ran a hand down her tail. She really was a mermaid.

With a thrust of her tail, she dove toward the kelp forest, winding through the long brown and gold leaves. Purple urchins lined the ocean floor and curious sea otters joined her, ducking in and out of cover.

Last night, she'd stayed up thinking of mermaids, Lon, George's offer, and Jenny's disappearance. She'd read all the pages Jenny marked with sticky notes in that odd book and she also looked up popular dive sites.

A short distance from here, near Snake Island, sat two old navy ships, the HMCS Cape Breton, a four-hundred-foot cape-class maintenance ship, and the HMCS Saskatchewan, a three-hundred-and-sixty-six-foot Mackenzie-class destroyer. Apparently, both artificial reefs teemed with life, and she'd spent the rest of the night refreshing her memory of the local marine flora and fauna around Gabriola.

Though Gabriola Pass and Dodd Narrows were closer, she knew from the locals talking and that those areas had powerful currents. She might not have to worry about drowning, but she didn't want to get stuck or swept away.

Willa headed toward the twin shipwrecks and reached the more northern placed vessel first—the HMCS Saskatchewan. The website wasn't kidding. Ocean life had covered every inch of the ship since the government scuttled it. The structure now looked more like another sandstone formation carved by the ocean than a navy destroyer.

Orange and white plumose anemones covered the metal surface along with barnacles and other invertebrates. Fish swam around the shipwreck as well—large yellow rockfish glowed in the lightening waters, sleek lingcod, silvery perch and scaleless cabezons with their spiny dorsal fins and broad mouths.

Willa swam with the sea life, enjoying the feel of her long hair flowing along her back in the cool current.

The HMCS Cape Breton materialized out of the ocean haze. Rusted metal covered in sea anemones and huge clusters of yellow cloud sponges shone in the sunlight streaking down from above. Brown and gold feather stars hung beside odd metal formations on sagging wire-railings. Rusticles. That's what they were called. Rusticles. She'd looked up the term when she first came across it during her research last night.

Her secret mermaid identity must've been why Dad never took her to the beach.

Dad knew.

Like a punch to the gut, the knowledge left her reeling and struggling to breathe.

Dad must've feared she'd discover her true nature. He'd freaked out when she took a diving course years ago. But why would he keep this from her? She'd missed a massive part of her life and hadn't realized it until this moment.

Willa would never lose this. The idea struck her and sent warmth through her body. Whether she stayed here or returned to Vancouver, she could visit the ocean. She could keep this. The ocean was her world now and all the memories she made here. Hers.

Beautiful, isn't it. Lon spoke from behind her.

She spun to face him, her hair flowing around her like a shield. *How did you find me?*

Lon floated a few feet away from her, a bioluminescent outline to mark his presence. The current flowed around him, adding dimension to his shape.

The ocean whispers. When rumours of a new Tritian swimming to Snake Island reached me, I knew it had to be you.

A Tritian. He'd called her that before. She dropped her arms from her chest. She didn't need to hide from Lon.

A mermaid or merman. It's a term used to describe any descendant of Triton.

Could Triton be my father?

Maybe. Or one of his sons. He has many, but only Aalton, Arran and Merrick are known to frequent these waters. The rest prefer more tropical regions. Aalton had a human lover decades ago. Went mad with grief when she disappeared.

Do you think Aalton's my father then?

Doubtful. His woman had a different name, and he hasn't taken a lover since. At least not that I know of. I am a lowly sprite, so anything is possible, and I'd be the last to know.

She drifted closer. *A lowly sprite?*

She sensed more than saw his smile. *It's practically blasphemy for me to talk with a princess of the sea.*

She flicked her tail to get even closer. In addition to

bouts of research, she'd spent a lot of time thinking about Lon. *I'm not a princess and you don't strike me as the type to stand on ceremony.*

His hands reached out and rested on her hips right above the first row of scales. *It sounds like you want to break some rules.*

Understatement of the year. *How many can we break?*

As many as you want. He pulled her into the heat of his presence.

Warmth continued to spread through her body, but how would this even work? *I don't know how mermaids do it,* she admitted.

Do it? Lon's form began to crystallize in the ocean and his eyes danced with humour as his fingertips trailed along her scales. His mouth crashed down on hers. Fisting his hand in her hair, he tilted her head back and deepened the kiss. Need spiraled up, flowing through her as Lon explored her body with his free hand. He hit a sensitive spot right where the apex of her legs would be if she still had them.

Oh!

She was already so hot, burning up with a need she couldn't quite understand. Lon slipped his finger into her, and she bucked in surprise. She had a hidden slit in her tail and Lon now worked it, pumping his finger in and out while he trailed kisses along her neck and breast. *Guess that answers my question.*

Lon smiled against her skin, but he seemed

distracted with moving his hand and setting her world on fire.

Fine then. Two could play that game. She reached between them, not certain with what she'd find in these altered states. Her hand brushed up against his hard length. *How are you taking human form?*

Instead of answering right away, Lon playfully caught her nipple between his teeth. *Would you like me to explain how you're accessing your mermaid powers and can now see me better or...?* He nipped at her other breast before swirling his tongue around the sensitive skin.

She groaned and dropped her head back. Her hair flowed in the water and exposed her pale skin in the streams of sunshine. Her chest thrust upward toward Lon's face, her breasts, full and heavy. She wanted more.

Lon's searing gaze met hers. *Do you like this?*

God, yes. She wrapped her hand around his hard length and moved her hand up and down.

Lon growled, capturing her mouth in a harsh, claiming kiss. He kissed her with a need and hunger she'd never experienced before. She continued to stroke him, enjoying the feel of his shaft and the zinging energy from the magic vibrating between them.

With his arm around her waist, he anchored her body to his and devoured her while the ocean around them flowed past, caressing her skin. Her head spun with rapture and—God yes, this. His tongue swirled, flicked, and licked, all the while kissing her, claiming her. And then suddenly, his mouth was gone, the heat replaced by the cold ocean water.

She cried out and opened her eyes. Her body ached with need.

Lon studied her as they bobbed in the ocean current. He didn't say anything, he didn't need to. He pulled her close, his hard shaft pressing against her throbbing entrance. He took her slowly at first, inching in, stretching her until he was all the way in. The pressure threatened to shatter her world, the sense of fullness exquisite.

His liquid gaze met hers, his gaze a swirl of storm clouds. *This is how mermaids do it.*

And then he began to move inside her.

CHAPTER
EIGHTEEN

"A love grown old holds summer's soul."

— ANGIE WEILAND-CROSBY

FIVE WEEKS AGO...

Jenny turned her face toward the angry sky, enjoying the mist of rain on her skin. Her niece would be here in two days and no amount of meditation, essential oils or distraction could ease her excitement. Things always seemed better with Willa—more vibrant, livelier.

Of course, getting that sweet girl away from her toxic ex and harpy of a mother were added bonuses.

The memory of her brother's face flashed in her mind and the pain of loss stabbed her gut. She smiled, a bittersweet smile. Her brother had been her idol. How someone so warm, funny and caring could fall for a she-devil still confused Jenny. But her brother had always been the faithful type. Loyal to a fault.

She stepped up on the next sandstone rock formation. Her foot pressed on a patch of green algae and slipped. Jenny whipped her arms around, windmilling, trying to regain her balance. Her foot slipped to join the other and the world tilted. She fell back. Her head slammed into the rock. Her vision wavered and darkened. She became weightless as she fell over the side and smacked the cold surface of the ocean.

Dark angry water engulfed her. She should fight. She should kick her legs, paddle with her arms. As darkness continued to creep onto her vision, her body drifted in the ocean. Her skin grew numb, and she no longer cared.

CHAPTER
NINETEEN

"At the beach, the heart opens a little wider."

— ANGIE WEILAND-CROSBY

CURRENT DAY...

Willa pulled her clothes on. The material stuck to her wet body. Her senses still hummed from Lon's touch, but her mind reeled. What was she doing? She didn't want to be an ocean princess of dubious lineage. The mermaid stuff was cool and all, but it wouldn't pay the bills. Could she spend her entire life in the ocean eating raw fish?

Her stomach twisted and she picked up her wet bathing suit to carry home.

The raw ocean diet didn't appeal to her, but most

importantly, it meant never getting answers about Jenny. Willa needed to stay grounded and focused.

The memory of Lon running his hands over her body warmed her skin. Staying focused didn't mean giving Lon up.

Her cheeks heated, no longer cold from the ocean. Memories of Lon could keep her warm during a snowstorm.

She tramped up the path, back to the road and headed toward home. She'd been gone most of the day —all Lon's fault, of course. The sunlight had begun to fade.

George sat on the front stoop, his elbows braced on his knees to hold his head up. He straightened when she approached and ran his hand through his hair.

Willa stopped short and studied her ex. His hair was messy, his shirt askew. He appeared dishevelled, which was so unlike him.

"Where have you been?" he asked.

Her cheeks warmed, but she refused to look away. "I needed some time to think."

"In the water?"

Her hair dripped with water and her clothing stuck to her damp skin. There was no point in denying where she'd been. "Best place to think."

Willa expected a tirade or at the very least a snide remark. Instead, he said, "Hungry?"

Her stomach rumbled. Yes, she was hungry and maybe a fully cooked meal would help clear her mind.

WILLA SAT across from George at the restaurant table and tried to mentally dissect his brain. The darkening sky and distant rumbles of thunder added to the intimate ambiance of their candle-lit dinner. He'd been a perfect gentleman all night; opening doors, pulling out chairs, and asking her questions. He'd even complimented her outfit, even though she was clearly underdressed in a simple blouse and pants that she'd tucked into tall gumboots.

George had laid on the charm and spared no cost. As if he weren't all that bad. As if he hadn't left her for Colleen. As if they were getting back together.

She wasn't falling for any of it.

George had been suitably charming when they first dated, as well, and that hadn't been an act. Had it? He'd never abused her physically, never physically mistreated her. He just needed to be in control. Be the man. But the hardest thing to come to terms with was, before he left her, she'd looked forward to their marriage, not for a way out.

"Willa?" George asked, his face pinching in.

"Sorry?"

"I wanted to know where you're at."

She sighed and placed her napkin neatly on the table. They'd enjoyed a five-course seafood feast and she might need to be rolled out of the restaurant. "Where I'm at with what?"

"With us."

"Oh." She glanced away, his gaze too intense. Nowhere. That's where she was, and she didn't intend to leave that place any time soon.

"Do you still care for me?"

"Well, yes..." She folded her hands on the tabletop.

"Do you still love me?"

She hesitated. Good question. Did she? "Love doesn't automatically switch off or on. It doesn't disappear. No one can control their heart with the flick of a switch," she said. "But you hurt me."

George exhaled a long breath, and, in that instant, a flash of that disgruntled expression crossed his face again. "Willa, I've apologized for that. It was a mistake and not one I plan to make again."

She nodded, more to her plate than him. Had he apologized, though? Truly? She didn't recall hearing the words, "I'm sorry." Her arms felt heavy. Too much food. Too much to process. She just wanted to go home and sleep.

"I'm going to make a decision," George said.

Her head snapped up and her brain smacked her skull. A headache bloomed. She hit her head often enough in the last few weeks to be the cause of her pain, but inherently, she knew it wasn't. No, this headache was George-induced.

Whenever George said he'd made a decision in the past, it meant he made plans for both of them. Plans she never liked. George leaned forward and clasped her hands in his, the movement so fast, she flinched.

"You love me, but you're hurt. I get that. I'm not saying things will go back to the way they were. Maybe that's a good thing. But I want to build a new relationship, from this point forward, and if you love me, you'll want the same thing."

Willa bit her lip. She tended to avoid conflict, but she didn't plan to condemn herself to a life with George just to avoid an uncomfortable conversation. Why couldn't he have stayed away?

"Let's go back to the house. You can pack your bags and lock up the shop. We can head out right away. Come home with me, Willa. It's where you belong." He spoke to her with the same tone he used for business transactions. Because that was what she was to him. A commodity.

"What about Jenny?" She couldn't bring herself to call her Aunt Jenny anymore, but Mom felt off, too.

"Did you discover anything these last few weeks? Find any clues?" He released her hands.

She opened her mouth and then shut it. What could she say? She learned mythical creatures existed, she was an adopted mermaid who did scandalous things with a water sprite, and she discovered Jenny was her biological mother and her biological father was probably ocean royalty? It sounded ridiculous to her own ears, and she didn't trust George with the truth.

George dabbed the corners of his mouth with a

napkin. "Your presence here isn't helping her. The only one benefitting is your mom. You know she's hoping to keep all the earnings from the store if Jenny never reappears. And you're the one working your ass off. Come back to Vancouver. I can support you, and if you don't want that, you could probably get your old job back. I know your boss; I can put in a good word for you."

"I just..."

"Need some time?" He nodded as if he'd anticipated her response.

That wasn't what she planned to say.

"You can have as much time as you want in Van," he continued. "And if you want, you can open Jenny's shop when the tourist season starts. I'll help you."

Going back to Van, to a life she knew very well, had its allure. A return to the familiar. The comfortable, the mundane. The inane. But running off to Van wouldn't change the very tangible reality that she could grow a tail and sprout gills. She pretended to consider his proposal, but she already knew the answer.

More memories of Lon's gaze with lightning and thunder filled her mind. She enjoyed her time with Lon and how he made her feel and how he made her skin sing. Maybe their relationship would turn into something more, given time. But Lon wasn't the reason she wanted to stay.

For the first time in her life, she truly felt like herself.

George studied her from across the table, his lips slightly turned up and his shoulders relaxed. His hands enfolded her own, warm and familiar.

"I'm not going back with you." She pushed away from the table. "Thank you for the meal and closure."

George opened and closed his mouth, confusion flashing across his face.

"Goodbye, George." And without looking back, she got up and walked away.

In addition to growing a tail, she'd finally found her backbone.

CHAPTER
TWENTY

"A sweet breeze and a patch of shade are the loveliest gifts on hot summer days."

— ANGIE WEILAND-CROSBY

A spasm clutched Willa's heart, leaving her hollow. She shuffled along the dark road, staring out at the sea and the darkening horizon. A haze had fallen over her mind, followed by numbness that didn't stop at the fingertips; instead, it ran along her arms and legs and settled in her chest, leaving her heavy and empty all at once. She had too much to process, and her mind had finally crashed like an ancient server.

The ocean rolled and curled under the increasing

wind. The forecast called for heavy showers and thirty percent chance of thunder and lightning. Not strong enough for Lon, not yet. What kind of life could they have together? Though technically she could live in the water, she had no desire to stay there. She couldn't read books and she'd have to eat seaweed and raw fish.

No, she couldn't live in the sea, and Lon couldn't survive on land. She'd already given up her dreams and ambitions for one man, she didn't plan to do that ever again.

So, what were her dreams and ambitions?

Silence answered her. Everyone had to have a goal in life and motivation to get there, right? What did it mean if she didn't have any?

She walked off the side of the road and climbed down to the water. Staying on Gabriola Island represented hope and independence, and at the same time delusion. Happy endings belonged in fairy tales.

Willa stepped into the cold water until it hit her boots mid-shin. The waves crashed before they reached her, but the push of the ocean still pressed against her calves. Maybe she should slip from her clothes, dive in and find Lon.

The wind howled, flinging her hair back and away from her face. Another monstrous wave crashed, and she staggered back a few steps. Maybe a late night swim wasn't such a good idea.

With a crash of thunder, a sheet of rain fell hard. In two seconds, Willa's clothes were soaked. She tilted her head up to the sky and revelled in the downpour of water against her face.

She should return to the shop. Talking about the future with Lon could wait for another day. With a deep breath and one last look at the churning dark ocean, Willa turned around to walk back to the bookstore.

Alice stood in her way. Normally coifed and well-dressed, Alice looked like her own rebellious twin. Her wild brown gaze reflected the flash of lightning overhead, and the wind whipped her gray-streaked hair around, making it come alive. "You should've stayed away."

"What?"

"That was the deal," Alice hissed.

"What deal?"

"A memory for a memory." Alice raised her hands and the waves surged in response. "You were never supposed to return. With your mother's memories erased and your adoptive family in place, you should've been content on the mainland."

A memory for a memory? Her mother's erased? Had Alice somehow made Jenny forget her own child? "Why...why would you do that?"

"A bargain made is a bargain done." Alice's hair whipped around her face. Banding together in thick parts, the tips melded together as if forming something else entirely. Not snakes, but...eels?

Willa blinked and leaned forward. "The sea witch?"

Alice quirked her lips too cruelly to be a smile.

Something hot burned in her pocket. She reached down and slipped her hand in to close around the hag stone. It burned her skin, but she held on, hoping it would provide the protection Ms. Murphy promised.

"What did you do?" Willa demanded. Had Alice made Jenny disappear?

"What your mother asked me to do."

Willa's stomach sunk. So Jenny had wanted to forget her. She'd purposefully asked for her memories to be erased and gave Willa to her brother. Willa sucked in a breath, her lungs suddenly feeling too tight. "And what do you plan to do now?"

"Jenny broke the spell." Her lips twisted as if she sucked on a lemon. "Or at least part of the spell. Some of it still remains."

"Did you hurt her? Is that why she's gone?"

"I don't know where she is, but luckily you arrived in her place to take the punishment." Alice brought her hands down. The ocean receded, but the air thrummed with power. "Jenny broke the spell, so now I'll break you."

Willa froze. What did she mean by that? Exactly how did she plan to break her with water? Did she not know Willa was a mermaid?

Before Willa could dive into the water and avoid whatever evil plan Alice intended, a blur of orange and red streaked between them. Ms. Murphy slammed into Alice with the power of a professional rugby player and knocked the other woman to the sandy ground.

"Off with ye, lass." The elderly woman screamed over her shoulder. "Go! Now."

Willa blinked and stood uselessly to the side as the two older women wrestled and rolled around in the wet sand.

"You insufferable woman," Alice hissed.

Ms. Murphy jabbed the sea witch in the side. For a brief moment, the Scottish woman looked up, perfectly timed in such a way that another streak of lightning illuminated her face. Instead of the elderly scowl Ms. Murphy often wore, an inhumanly beautiful face with smooth skin and dancing green eyes looked back at her.

Willa sucked in a breath. Fae. Willa's mind connected the dots and as if time paused for this moment, Ms. Murphy met her gaze and winked. "I've got this, lass."

A fae fought a sea witch to save a mermaid. When exactly had her life taken such a left turn?

The moment broke. With the lighting gone, Ms. Murphy's wrinkled old face returned, and the women continued to grunt, roll, and smack each other while hissing profanities.

Willa turned and ran from the beach. She might not be the sharpest tool in the shed, but at least she knew when to run.

CHAPTER
TWENTY-ONE

"She beats to the beauty of her wildflower heart and seashore soul."

— ANGIE WEILAND-CROSBY

Fuck this. Willa threw her clothing into the suitcase with force. She might've been adamantly against returning to Vancouver before her little beach visit, but now her mind was made up. She didn't have any skills or knowledge to battle a sea witch.

Alice had attacked her, and Willa didn't plan to stick around and find out exactly how Alice planned to break her as a punishment for Jenny's actions. Now back at the shop, she had time to collect her thoughts and her things.

Having fled to Gabriola, she'd arrived with very little. Since then, she'd accumulated enough clothes to need a second suitcase. She pulled out one of Aunt Jenny's and stared at the case.

She let out another big sigh.

"Willa, are you here?" George's voice travelled up the stairs.

She froze. What the hell was he doing here? She couldn't have been clearer with her rejection.

The front door slammed shut and boots smacked against the flooring, growing louder as each second passed.

"Why are you here?" she yelled back.

"I'm taking you back to Van," he growled. "I won't take no for an answer."

Ugh. What a tool. She'd have to get rid of him and then escape to the ferry. Willa threw the last shirt into her luggage. Staring at her full suitcase, strange numbness travelled across her skin. All she had to do was reach out and close the hard-shelled case.

Her feet grew roots into the old wood flooring.

She lifted her arm and leaned forward, but an invisible weight burdened her limbs and it fell lifeless to her side. She breathed in and out. *I'm doing the right thing.* She reached out again to close the suitcase with her other arm, but it fell back to her side unsuccessful, as well.

She couldn't do it.

She couldn't leave this place.

She couldn't leave Lon or Jenny.

Maybe Lon could help her find a way to neutralize the sea witch.

"Willa, for fuck's sake, say something," George bellowed. With each word, she heard him stomp up the stairs until he entered her room. He halted just inside the doorway, his gaze flicking between her and the packed suitcase. "Oh, good. You're already packing."

"I can't do this," she said. Her plans to flee to Vancouver faded away and left her elated, like she'd been wearing shoulder pads of solid lead only to have the sun melt them away.

"Just close the fucking case, Willa. Simple." His tone turned darker, and his body tensed.

"No. I can't do this." She turned and waved her hand at the suitcase. "I'm not going to Vancouver with you."

"And what if you change your mind after I've left? Just finish packing, Willa. We'll talk about it on the ferry."

Willa's muscles tensed. He never used that tone unless he was pissed. She shook her head. "I won't change my mind. I don't want to spend another minute with you. Leave. And don't even think of letting yourself back into this bookstore without permission or *accidentally* missing the last ferry to stay another night."

Though her head still reeled from everything she

discovered on the island, and there was the pesky problem of an angry sea witch to deal with, she'd never felt more alive.

After she got this jerk out the door, she'd go to the ocean, transform and find Lon.

"You little bitch!" George visibly shook. He took a menacing step forward and raised his arm to strike her.

Willa's breath hitched. She clenched her jaw, straightened her back, and prepared to fight.

"Touch her and die," a stormy voice crashed through the room.

Lon!

A surge of energy flowed through Willa's body and wiped out her tension.

She stepped to the side and beamed at Lon.

George stiffened before turning to see the newcomer—a large, powerful man, ready to pommel him to death.

George looked insignificant compared to Lon. Her ex's gaze darted back and forth from her to Lon. His brain probably calculating the likelihood of outcomes.

Judging from the rage streaking across Lon's face, none of the possibilities were good for him.

"Fuck this," George muttered. He shouldered past Lon and stomped down the stairs. "You're not worth it."

The tension from her shoulders eased with each step George took away from her. Willa held her breath until the front door slammed. She turned to Lon, and a different emotion flooded her body. Hope.

Willa and Lon moved toward each other at the same time.

Lon stepped forward and crumpled.

Willa lunged forward and caught Lon. His heavy body smacked into hers and her legs buckled. They crashed to the ground, with Lon's weight pinning her to the floor.

"Been here." She laughed when she caught her breath. The flowing energy unique to him travelled up her arm and embraced her heart. The sense of home flooded her body. "I'm glad you came."

Lon's chest rumbled, but no laughter came out. "You were planning on leaving?"

"Not anymore." She hesitated. "Did you see the sea witch?"

"That crazy old bat." He nodded and smiled. "I came because I saw how scared you were. You have nothing to fear from the sea witch."

"But she's a sea witch."

"Whose most powerful skill is calling the tides. You can't drown, remember?" Lon pushed up on shaking forearms and used his trembling thumbs to caress her face. His smile sweet and tender. Yet, something was wrong. Why did he look so weak?

She glanced outside. Wind? Check. Rain? Check.

Thunder? Not for a while. Same with the lightning. In terms of West Coast storms, the one outside was mild to negligible.

She turned back to Lon's stormy eyes. The understanding scooped out her heart and left her numb. "There's no storm."

Lon nodded, a bare twitch of his chin up and down.

"I thought you'd run away. I needed to stop you, or at least see you before you left." His arms trembled against hers. "It took everything to form and come to you. My power is almost gone."

"Why...Why would you do that?"

"Do you not hear it?" Lon asked abruptly.

She paused and listened. Aside from the normal sounds, she didn't hear a thing. "Hear what?"

"My heart."

She smiled and shook her head.

"It beats for you, Willa. If you left, a part of me would leave with you." He ran his thumb over her cheek. "I'm glad you're staying."

He collapsed on top of her, and she felt more than heard his deep sigh, a labored breath of contentment.

She cradled him in her arms. This couldn't be happening. She'd finally kicked George to the proverbial curb, and Lon saved her. She should feel euphoric, but the one thing she craved most was getting ripped away from her.

Icy fingers wrapped around her thudding heart and

tugged. "I don't understand. I don't know what's happening."

She gripped his cheeks and gently pushed his head back to stare into the depths of his gaze. His lips twitched into a smile, but the waves of energy from him diminished. The wane of his power left her cold and numb. Thunderclouds ceased circling in his irises. They changed to dull slated gray.

Her heart hammered in her chest.

"No." Tears leaked from her eyes, and she blinked them away. "Please don't leave me."

She leaned forward and pressed her lips to his. Lon's mouth moved into a fuller smile under her lips, and her body tingled as a wave of warmth moved through her body to his, as if their very kiss pulled energy from her body. Then he angled his head, opened his mouth and deepened the kiss.

The window of her bedroom flew open; gusts of strong ocean wind blew into the room. The mirror on the wall crashed to the floor, the lamp beside the bed shattered. Rain soaked all her stuff, but she didn't care. She stared into the deep stormy pools of Lon's eyes. They clouded, like the sky outside gathering before thunder and lightning. The swirling gray danced around and hypnotized her, drawing energy until Lon glowed.

She gasped as the wind and rain bore down on her through the window. The power of the elements surged into her body and steeped her in energy until she hummed with power, both floating and heavy at the same time. It flowed through her veins and poured into her soul.

Her vision flashed white and orange like a lightning strike.

Then, the crushing force softened, weakening, but not leaving her empty. It flowed out of her body and into Lon. Light continued to flood him, making his skin glow and illuminate the room with glittering cascades of blue, white and silver light. His ink-black hair framed his face and enhanced his pale skin and otherness. He was the most beautiful thing she'd ever laid eyes on.

"We have about thirty minutes before I need to get back to the ocean," he said.

She licked her lips and raked his body with her gaze. "I think I have an idea of how we can spend that time."

"You might need to revive me again if you're thinking what I'm thinking."

She leaned forward and kissed him again. When she finally pulled back to breathe, she traced his lips with her fingertips. "I'll revive you as many times as we need."

"You accessed more of your power." Lon's gaze sparked with his internal lightning. "How do you feel?"

"Like I'm finally home."

CHAPTER
TWENTY-TWO

"The sun's love affair with summer perfumed every inch of her warm soul."

— ANGIE WEILAND-CROSBY

FIVE WEEKS AGO...

Jenny woke with her cheek squished against wet rock. Her whole body ached. She groaned and peeled her face from the surface. Her wet clothes clung to her body and the ocean water plastered her hair to the sides of her face.

Her head throbbed. She'd really whacked it. Blinking hard a couple of times, the pain subsided enough for her to take in her surroundings. Evidently, she was in some sort of underwater cave. Dim light pierced the darkness from cracks and holes above. Rain slipped in and splattered against the rock.

She'd hit her head and somehow arrived here. How? The current couldn't have pulled her here.

And how did she get out?

A quiet *slap, slap, slap,* echoed in the chamber and grew a little louder. Not rain drops like she assumed.

She rolled over and instantly regretted it. The room swam. She reached out and braced herself, waiting for the wave of nausea to flow away.

Someone paced in the room.

Her vision cleared and Jenny gulped.

Stalking back and forth a few feet away was a large, very naked man. Ocean water trickled from him, trailing the hard planes of his sculpted body.

The smell of wet dirt, ocean water and seaweed curled around her. Something pinged in her mind, like a memory trying to poke its way to the surface. She scrambled to her feet and clenched her teeth as another wave of nausea hit. Maybe she should've stood slower.

The man whirled toward her. His eyes widened. "Are you okay?"

She blinked at him. She'd expected him to say something more serial-killer-ish.

"How are you feeling?" he asked.

Oh, my dear lord, his voice was hypnotizing. She could listen to him speak all day.

He watched her and waited for a response.

"Confused," she answered honestly.

His platinum eyebrows drew down.

"How did I get here?"

"I brought you." He clenched his hands into fists.

She took a step back. "Why?"

"You fell into the water and hit your head. You're lucky I happened to be nearby," he continued. "I don't often come this way. Not anymore, but sometimes... sometimes I pass by, just in case."

"In case of what?" That wasn't the right question. She should be asking something else, but the man intrigued her.

He tilted his head at her and in that moment, looked so...not human. Ethereal, unearthly, other-worldly. Fae-like.

"In case I found you again. I kept searching, even after all these years. But I never felt you in the water." His bright blue-green gaze dimmed as though an invisible cloud passed over him. "I suspected you avoided the ocean by choice and though I respected your wishes, it didn't stop me from hoping."

Jenny blinked at the man again. He might be the most handsome human being she'd ever seen, but clearly, he was also delusional. She had no idea what he was talking about. Maybe the nudist colony had started to experiment with drugs. "I'm sorry. But who are you?"

The man rocked back on his heels, his soft, vulnerable expression gone. "Are you saying you don't know me?"

She shook her head and bit her lip. "I think I'd remember you."

"That isn't funny Skye."

Huh? "I haven't gone by Skye since I was... Oh hell, I don't even remember when the last time was. Probably not since I was eighteen."

The man paled. "Do you remember anything from when you were eighteen?"

She shrugged. "Not much to remember."

He flinched.

"I finished high school, worked over the summer on the island and then went to college," she explained. Pretty ordinary events for an eighteen-year-old.

"And?" His muscles remained taut, as if tension had wound him up tighter and tighter.

"And it wasn't for me. I made it through one semester and decided academia wasn't my thing. I hadn't saved as much as I'd hoped and had to work anyway."

He grunted. "I meant, do you remember anything else? Anything about me and this cave?"

She balked. "I've never seen you or this cave before."

Wet dirt, ocean water, seaweed...

Something about the way this place smelled was familiar to her.

He stalked forward.

"Eep." Jenny stumbled back, her feet kicking up water.

The man froze, horrified. "I would never hurt you."

"You're a powerful man who's kidnapped me to a secure, remote location." She glanced down and sucked in a breath. She tore her gaze away. "And you're naked."

He glowered and stepped forward again, grabbing her arm with quick reflexes. He didn't squeeze. He didn't haul her to him. Instead, he settled that mesmerizing blue-green gaze on her, a small smile tugging at his lips. "Just hold still. I suspect some sort of spell has been placed on you."

"Spell?" she scoffed. "There's no such thing."

The man placed his palm on her forehead and closed his eyes. Wind whipped around the cave and the storm outside howled. A tingling sensation travelled through her head, warm and not unpleasant. It reached a dark shadowy area and as if there were a door there, the tingling sensation wrapped around the handles and tore it open.

Wet dirt, ocean water, seaweed...

The memories rushed forward. Beach time, hot summers, long swims and mermaids. Mermen. Tritians.

Prince Aalton, youngest son of King Triton.

Heat flamed her cheeks as more memories of the man standing in front of her surged forward, ones of him splaying her against this very shore, savouring the taste of her skin, pumping into her, worshipping her body.

"Aalton?" she whispered.

His blue-green gaze brightened.

Then another memory punched her in the gut, rocking her to the core. A memory so precious and painful, it took her insides and twisted them into a knot while simultaneously sucking her breath away. Her chest constricted. Her lungs burned. She couldn't breathe. Jenny doubled over from the memories. "Oh god. Oh god. What have I done?"

Aalton reached forward, concern etched in his brow. "What is it?"

"Willa."

Aalton blinked at her. "Who?"

Her stomach sunk lower, and more memories flooded in, memories held back the invisible wall placed in her mind by the sea witch. She staggered to the side.

Aalton reached forward and gripped her elbow to steady her. His ocean green gaze scanned her face. "The spell still clings to your soul. We need to get you to my father. I do not have the ability to heal the damage."

She locked her knees and shook her head. "No. I...I need to get back."

"You will not survive if I leave you like this." He hesitated. "Will this Willa survive without you?"

Jenny swayed, Aalton's firm grip the only thing preventing her from toppling over. "She'll worry."

"That's survivable."

"You don't understand. She's...she's my daughter." Jenny fumbled through her memories, her head pounded, and her vision closed in. "Our daughter."

Aalton stiffened, his grip dug into her arm. His brows became two angry slashes, and he pressed his lips together hard enough that they formed a straight line.

"Please don't kill her." Jenny's vision continued to close in, Aalton's beautiful face becoming fuzzy and faded as darkness descended.

"I will cherish our daughter," Aalton said. "But first, you need to heal."

EPILOGUE

"I wade in her droplets of mystery; my soul one with the wild charmed sea."

— ANGIE WEILAND-CROSBY

CURRENT DAY...

The smell of garlic, chocolate and patchouli drifted on the breeze as the heat of the summer day bore down on Willa's covered head. She strolled with Lon, hand in hand through the busy vendors in the market. Her newfound mermaid skills allowed her to see auras, and she relished watching the vibrant colours of her neighbours and the tourists dance around. Each time she came back from a swim, her skills improved.

They'd spent the day sampling food at the market.

With bellies full of treats, they ambled to the bookstore they now ran together. A month ago, they'd completed a bonding ceremony that made life on land easier for Lon and allowed them to stay closer. The bond could be reversed, but Willa couldn't imagine her life without Lon.

Not like her mother. Her adoptive mother. She'd cut that vile woman from her life and felt ten years younger and one-hundred and forty pounds lighter. Good riddance.

Willa pressed her spare hand to her over-stuffed stomach. "I'm so full. You might have to carry me the rest of the way."

Lon smiled and bent to kiss her temple. "I'm sure we can think of ways to work off all this food. Which dish was your favorite?"

"Definitely the fudge."

"Mine, too."

He squeezed her hand with his own and they continued to walk.

They turned the corner to find Alice standing at the side of the road. Willa tensed, but Lon continued his easy pace.

The sea witch looked over at them and scowled.

Instead of running away, like Willa's instincts told her to, she raised her hand and waved.

Alice scowled harder.

Lon laughed and tugged Willa along. Just like her previous run-ins with Alice, this one didn't result in her demise. Whatever Ms. Murphy had said or done, she'd ensured the sea witch remained on her best behaviour.

Before she discovered Alice's true identity, Willa had always assumed Alice kind of took care of Ms. Murphy. But nope. It was the other way around. The fae woman kept the sea witch on a short leash.

A gust of ocean air blew across Willa's face and flung her hair in all directions. Holding hands never carried this much joy for her until now. As long as she touched or kissed Lon frequently, he could maintain his human form without the need of a storm.

She'd forever cherish the memory of his expression when he first stood in the middle of the street during a hot summer's day, his eyes wide, and his mouth open in amazement.

She saw the other sprites now, too. Lon hadn't lied when he spoke about his brothers. Due to their long lives, they often drifted apart, but also, due to the cyclical nature of the tides, and life in general, they drifted back together again. She'd had a few over for dinner during the last storm and now understood why Lon didn't mind his moments of solitude.

A bunch of his brothers played in the waves in their malleable tempest forms. They were thin as reeds; wisp-like as smoke; playful as leaves in a light breeze; a streak of blue, silver and white, human in form, but bending, elongating and curling with each roll and wave of the ocean. They existed in simplicity without malice, entirely filled with joy.

"Do you miss that?" she asked. "Playing in the waves with your brothers?"

He shrugged. "I can splash in the water whenever I want, and I see my brothers often enough. I find life on land thoroughly enjoyable."

"Maybe we could go for a swim later," she suggested. They'd reached the shop and she unlocked the door.

"I'd like that." Lon opened the door and held it open for her.

She stepped into the store and let the familiar smell of books wash over her while Lon closed the door. He swooped her into a hug and kissed her neck. His erection pressing into her backside told her what he'd also like to do right about now.

Footsteps up the stairs outside interrupted her thoughts.

"We're closed," Lon growled over his shoulder before going back to her neck.

The handle turned and the door jiggled.

Lon released her with a sigh and they both turned toward the front entrance. As the door swung open, Lon took a step forward and placed his body slightly in front of hers.

A woman stood in the doorway. Short and petite with a lean body that defied her age of forty-eight, the woman's thick blonde hair blew forward with the gust of ocean air and covered her flushed, radiant skin and piercing blue eyes. Her gold and purple aura swirled around her like a cape, reaching forward to tangle with her own. It sparkled as if containing millions of diamond dust particles. Willa couldn't fully view her own aura, only sense its presence, but if it looked anything like this, no wonder Lon kept staring at her and smiling.

Jenny beamed at Willa. Mom. Her mother.

"I'm so sorry, Willa." Jenny's unsure expression twisted Willa's heart. "I...I needed time to heal. I couldn't come back right away. Staying away, knowing you'd worry, knowing I left without an explanation hurt me almost as much as my memories and the healing process. I think you and I need to sit down and talk. I have things...I have things I need to tell you."

Willa had so many questions.

But answers could wait. Jenny was home. Willa stepped around Lon to embrace her aunt.

And stopped.

A dark silhouette moved in behind Jenny and placed a large protective hand on her hip. The air sucked out of the room, taking all the sound with it. Willa tensed at the large foreboding figure in front of her.

Jenny had come home, all right. And she wasn't alone. With blond, shoulder-length hair and a tall imposing figure, the man standing in front of her certainly made an impression. It took a few extra seconds to register that he wore ripped ill-fitting jeans and a shirt a few sizes too small. Water dropped from his hair as if he's recently stepped from the ocean.

The man bowed. "Greetings, Willa."

"H-h-hello," she stuttered.

Lon froze beside her. He looked torn between running and fighting. Instead of fleeing from her side, he straightened and pulled his shoulders back. He reached out and grabbed her hand.

"My name is Aalton. Prince Aalton." His voice was deep and gravely, like the roar of large waves before they crashed against the shore. "I'm the youngest son of King Triton and grandson of Poseidon, but most importantly, I'm your father."

"Our memories of the ocean will linger on, long after our footprints in the sand are gone."

— UNKNOWN

Acknowledgments

I spent a lot of my formative years living on Gabe and know the island well. Despite this, I still might've got some things wrong and I definitely took some creative licence for the location of the bookstore. There is no 3000 square foot shipwright's mansion near Twin Beaches Market, formerly known as the B&K. Any mistakes for the locations on the island are my own.

To my wonderful critique partners: Jo-Ann Carson, Charlotte Copper and Shelly Chalmers...

To my beta readers Kristi Kyle, Jackelyn Ford, Karilyn Bentley, Wendy P and Cassie Patterson...

To the Lobster Cove crew for letting me be a part of the creation process for the original short story from which *Call of the Deep* arose...

To my former publisher, the Wild Rose Press for picking up the original version of this story...

To my cover artist, Andrea, from CReya-tive Book Cover Design for creating a beautiful cover...

To my editor and fellow science geek, Lara Parker...

To my supportive family, amazing friends, and my wonderful in-laws...

To my readers...

Thank you.

Your support and feedback mean the world to me. May your joys be as deep as the oceans, and your troubles as light as its foam.

ABOUT THE AUTHOR

J. C. McKenzie is a book loving, gumboot-wearing, unapologetic science geek. She predominantly writes urban fantasy and post-apocalyptic dystopian fantasy with strong romantic elements. When she's not spinning tales, she's in the classroom sharing her passion for science and mathematics while secretly warping the young, impressionable minds of our future to carry out her evil plans for world domination. She lives in the Pacific Northwest with her family.

Visit her at jcmckenzie.ca

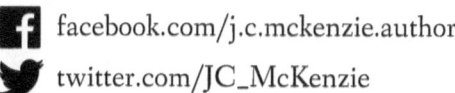

facebook.com/j.c.mckenzie.author

twitter.com/JC_McKenzie

instagram.com/j.c.mckenzie